IT WAS HARD TO BELIEVE
THERE WAS ANY DANGER IN THIS.

It was a game, a big joke they were going to play on some unsuspecting stranger.

"Like some coffee?" she asked Kobelski.

"Sounds good. I've got a long night ahead."

She got up and turned toward the tiny kitchenette.

"Don't do that!"

Lauren whirled around to look at him. The detective stood up and gave her a fierce look. The scar on his left cheek stood out in a ragged white line.

"What's wrong?" she asked, frightened.

"You turned your back on me!" His teeth were clenched in anger. "I warned you not to do that!"

Lauren felt dizzy. "But you—I—I can trust *you!*"

His expression was still grim. "This is no game, Lauren! From now on, you trust *no one.*"

ANDREA HARRIS
A Scream Away

PLAYBOY PRESS
PAPERBACKS

A SCREAM AWAY

Cover illustration by George Gaadt.

Published simultaneously in the United States and Canada by Playboy Press, Chicago, Illinois. Printed in the United States of America. Library of Congress Catalog Card Number: 78-62017. First edition.

This book is available at quantity discounts for promotional and industrial use. For further information, write our sales promotion agency: Ventura Associates, 40 East 49th Street, New York, New York 10017.

ISBN: 0-872-16510-8

CHAPTER ONE

Afterward, Lauren realized that he must have been waiting for her. She had just returned to her apartment, dropped her books onto the tiny table in the alcove which served as an eating area, and flung her sweater onto the sofa when she heard a soft rap on the door.

She hesitated before answering. It wasn't her landlady's businesslike knock. Lauren had only moved in a month before and didn't know anyone else who might be visiting her at ten o'clock on a Wednesday night.

"Who is it?" She raised her voice in order to be heard clearly through the massive oak door, one of the building's many reminders of more gracious living in its earlier days.

"Detective Kobelski, Miss Walker. May I speak with you?"

A detective? Lauren's first thought was of her mother. She heard her pulse pounding in her ears as she unlocked the door. *Oh, dear God! Not another suicide attempt!*

"My mother! Is she all right?" she gasped.

The man who stood in the hall was tall, broad-shouldered, and muscular with a square jaw. He flashed an identification card.

"Your mother is fine as far as I know," he said softly. "I didn't mean to alarm you."

Before she could react, he stepped past her into the apartment.

"Then what do you want?" Lauren was suddenly apprehensive. He wasn't dressed like a detective. His brown plaid sport coat was shapeless and wrinkled, and he wore no tie. His face, however, was ruggedly attractive despite a ragged scar that ran from the top of his left cheekbone to his ear.

He glanced around the room. Lauren had the feeling that nothing escaped him: shabby brown sofa only half disguised by a colorful afghan; cheerful travel posters covering peeling wallpaper; scattering of small potted plants struggling to bring life into the little apartment.

"What do you want?" she asked again. If he hadn't come about Ma, why was he here? She had no one else. She was suddenly frightened. She shouldn't have let him in. That's what came from having grown up in a small town. She didn't distrust strangers automatically.

"Why don't we sit down?" he suggested. "This may take a while." Without waiting for her reply, he strode over to the sofa and, stretching his long legs out in front of him, eased his large frame onto it.

Trying to stifle her misgivings, Lauren drew out a straight-backed chair from the little table in the alcove. She positioned it so that if he made any move toward her, she could dash for the door.

"I've got a business proposition for you, Miss Walker," the big man was saying softly.

"Me?" Lauren looked at him. "You must have the wrong person. I'm new in town. What could you know about me?"

"I know that your name is Lauren Marie Walker. You're twenty-two years old and work full time as a research technician at the Kincaid Institute under Dr. Maxwell Herbert. I know that you're going to the university part time. You're working toward a master's degree in immunology and hope eventually to get a Ph.D."

She stared at him uneasily. He was right about everything.

"I know that you're the only child of Frank and Mary Walker, originally from Waterville," he went on in a monotone. "Your father deserted you and your mother when you were three. The two of you lived with your grandmother until her death. Your mother is fairly unstable, has had a periodic drinking problem and now lives with her sister in Florida."

"How do you know all that?"

"I'm a detective," Kobelski said gently. "It's my business to know everything I can about anyone I'm going to hire."

"I don't understand." Lauren's mind was racing. Was he mentally unbalanced? Or some kind of con artist? What would she do if he refused to leave? If she screamed, would anyone come to her rescue?

Certainly not elderly Mr. Emerson, who lived across the hall. In the apartment above lived the Petries, a young couple with two small daughters. But Mr. Petrie worked nights—he wasn't home at this hour. The only other person in the building was the landlady, Mrs. Harper, who lived on the third floor.

"Have you ever heard of Diane Towle or Ellen Rickover?" Kobelski was asking her.

She frowned, then shook her head. "I don't think so."

"They were murdered—strangled—here in the city within the last two-and-a-half months," he said.

A vague memory began untangling itself in her mind.

"I may have heard something on the radio about the Rickover murder," she said slowly. "It was shortly after I moved here, wasn't it?" She shook her head. "I don't get a newspaper regularly and I don't own a TV, so I'm not up on the local news."

Kobelski smiled. He had a nice smile, she thought. One that made it hard not to like him.

"No papers, no TV? That makes you pretty unusual."

"Just short of money and time," Lauren retorted defensively.

"I know that, too. You'd really like to quit your job and go to school full time, wouldn't you?"

She wanted it so much that it hurt to hear the words spoken aloud. The way things were going now, it would be four or five years before she got her master's degree. Beyond that, she couldn't see. It was next to impossible to work for a Ph.D. in a science on a part-time basis, but without financial support she couldn't become a full-time student. She had tried to get some assistance—a grant or a scholarship—from the university, but everywhere she turned, the story was the same. "Money is tight now."

Thinking about it made her irritated. "Mr. Kobelski, it's late and I have to go to work in the morning. Will you please get to the point?"

He smiled again. "Sorry. I do wander. The point is, Thomas Rickover hired me to find out who killed his daughter."

"You're a *private* detective, then?"

He nodded.

Maybe he *was* for real. "Go on."

"I'm pretty sure Ellen Rickover and Diane Towle were killed by the same person."

"What makes you think that?" Lauren asked, wondering what any of this had to do with her.

"A number of reasons. Each girl was killed in her own apartment. No signs of forced entry. Both were strangled by hand. That's unusual, you know. Most strangulations involve a piece of clothing or maybe a wire. And the bruises on the girls' necks were positioned almost identically."

He stopped and looked at Lauren for a long moment. "But the clincher is that both girls were the same physical type: small-boned, slender, with short blond hair, a rather long neck, a heart-shaped face, and wide-set eyes. They looked enough alike to be sisters."

Lauren suddenly shivered. "A psychopath? Do you think it's one man who's killing the same kind of woman over and over?"

Kobelski nodded. "And if I'm right, he's going to kill again—soon."

Her hands were cold, and she was trembling.

"I've been looking for a likely victim," he went on. He was watching her closely.

"And this business proposition you're offering me— what is it?" She fought to keep her voice steady. She believed she already knew the answer. Except for their short blond hair, his description of the dead women fitted her.

"I need bait. I'd want you to make a couple of changes in

your appearance and be seen a lot around campus. That's all.''

"That's all!'' She nearly shouted. "You've got a very casual attitude about my life, Mr. Kobelski! Give me one good reason why I should get involved in this''—she groped for the right word—"this *bizarre* scheme of yours!''

It was as if he'd been waiting for that question. "I can give you two reasons,'' he said softly. "First, you look like the dead women. I had no trouble spotting the resemblance, and the killer could, too.''

"What about my hair?''

"You're close enough.''

He let a silence stretch out between them. Finally he said, "Wouldn't you really prefer a bodyguard?''

Her stomach felt queasy. "What's the second reason?''

He made a tent with his large hands and stared at his fingertips. "Mr. Rickover is very wealthy. I've been authorized to make you an offer.''

"Which is?''

"Tuition, room, and board, plus a generous personal allowance for as long as you wish to continue your education.''

She stared at him in disbelief. "That could amount to a lot of money,'' she said slowly.

"Money doesn't mean much to Rickover. He just wants to get the guy who killed his daughter.''

For as long as you wish to continue your education. It was as if someone had asked her what one thing she wanted most. She couldn't remember a day when she hadn't wanted to go to school. From kindergarten on, school was a haven, a wonderful world filled with new things to do and learn. And a blessed time away from an embittered mother who soured every moment spent in her presence.

It hadn't been so bad while Gram was alive. A soft, warm, cheerful person, she had taken care of Lauren while Ma was at work. But after Gram died, things got worse. Ma's depressions deepened and her drinking became a real problem.

By the time she was in junior high, Lauren realized that

school, which had begun as an escape from home, had evolved into her main interest in life. She took it for granted that she would go to school for as long as possible. She graduated as valedictorian of her high school class. That earned her a tuition scholarship to a nearby college, where she studied while still living at home.

It was not an ideal situation. She would have preferred to go away to school. There was nothing easy about living with a woman whose whole purpose in life had walked out on her fifteen years earlier. Mary Walker had never forgiven fate for her lot. Nor did she ever miss an opportunity to remind anyone around her about it. Lauren couldn't count the number of times she had heard what an irresponsible, cruel, untrustworthy man her father had been. She tried to close her ears to such remarks and to harden herself against the hurt of her mother's words.

During those four years of college, she assumed quite blithely that she would go away to graduate school. Her grades were excellent; surely she could get a fellowship somewhere.

But when she began applying for financial support, the terrible truth became plain. Excellent grades at a small college like State didn't impress a graduate school faculty. Despite her problems, Ma had always managed to keep a steady job. And though there wasn't enough money at home to send Lauren away to school, they couldn't be considered poverty-stricken. So Lauren wasn't eligible for assistance on those grounds, either.

After several months of futile letter-writing, visits to several university campuses, and frustrating meetings with admissions directors, Lauren had to face the painful fact that if she wanted to continue her schooling, it could only be on a part-time basis. She would have to work to support herself. It would take forever to achieve that Ph.D. She could still taste the bitterness of that realization.

Kobelski pulled out his wallet from an inside pocket and peeled five crisp bills from it. He laid them on the little yellow parsons table that stood in front of the sofa. Five one-hundred-dollar bills.

"Expense money," he said softly. "To get your hair done, buy some new clothes. And I want you to eat out a lot. Keep yourself highly visible."

"I haven't said I'd do it."

"That's true."

But he made no move to pick up the money. He leaned back and relaxed, putting his arms out along the back of the sofa. His jacket fell open, exposing a shoulder holster and gun.

For a long moment, they stared at each other.

"Tell me about the—the women who were killed," Lauren said finally.

He shrugged. "The Towle girl was killed in July. She was pretty, just twenty-one. Worked as a barmaid at the Nite Owl. Ever hear of it?"

She nodded. "It's a student hangout near campus."

"She wanted to be a singer. Took voice lessons. Left home at eighteen, wasn't close to her family, no regular boyfriend."

"Did she live alone?"

"Ah-huh. Two rooms above a novelty shop near campus. Like I said, no sign of forced entry and not much struggle. He was someone she trusted, and he took her by surprise."

"And the other girl? What was her name—Ellen?"

"A university sophomore. Bright. Only seventeen. Studying art. The essential details are the same."

Was it her imagination, or was there a slight change in his voice when he mentioned the Rickover girl?

His face was impassive. "Well, what do you think?"

She stared at the money on the table. "I guess I want to know how much danger I'd be in and how you intend to protect me."

She saw a glint of satisfaction come into his eyes, and for a moment she wondered if he saw her as a fish to be played until his hook was set.

"Nothing could be simpler. Except for the time you're actually in class or at work, I'll be your bodyguard. You won't see me. I'll just melt into the background."

"And what if there's trouble?"

"Just remember: Don't turn your back on any man when you're alone with him. That gives you time to scream. I'll never be more than a scream away."

He stood up. "Is it a deal?"

Do I trust him, or don't I? Lauren looked at the one-hundred-dollar bills and then at Kobelski. He was big. And he had a gun. If he'd always be nearby, she couldn't be in too much danger, could she?

"It's a deal."

CHAPTER TWO

He had gone, but the money was still there on the table. Lauren picked up the bills and stared at them. This was only the beginning, he'd said. He'd handed over the five hundred as casually as if it had been five dollars. He wasn't kidding.

For a moment, she felt misgivings. What if something went wrong?

Abruptly, she interrupted her train of thought. She'd already made up her mind to do it. And there was only one way to succeed. Think positively. Think about going to school without having to pinch pennies.

She looked around her apartment. Except for that yellow plastic table that she had bought at Woolworth's, the furniture consisted of odds and ends from home. Ma had sold the better pieces to raise cash after she finally decided to move in with Lauren's Aunt Lil. No one had wanted this stuff. The shabby brown sofa with worn spots on the arms. The faded green easy chair with its broken springs. The ugly bookcase that some amateur carpenter had made long ago. The corners weren't squared and it wasn't sturdy enough to stand upright without leaning against the wall.

It would be nice to replace these things. To live in a cheerful-looking apartment.

And wouldn't it be nice to be able to study without the pressure of a job? In the daytime when she was rested, instead of late at night after a full day's work?

She folded the bills carefully and tucked them into her wallet. She'd deposit the money in her checking account tomorrow after work. She'd make an appointment then to have her hair cut and lightened.

Before he left, Kobelski had shown her photos of the two dead women. "I suggest you do your hair more like the

Rickover girl,'' he said. ''Miss Towle was a bit flamboyant. Okay for an entertainer, but I don't think it's you.''

He was right, of course. The picture of Diane showed a young woman with a short but elaborate hairdo with lots of little curls framing her face. It was a style that Lauren could never have worn comfortably.

Her first reaction upon seeing Ellen Rickover's picture was one of shock. The girl in the photo appeared both younger and older than she had expected. She was very pretty. Her complexion was smooth and clear, her eyes wide and untroubled beneath long lashes. In the set of her chin, Lauren saw a determined young woman who knew who she was and what she wanted. And at the same time, there was an air of vulnerability, the sweetness of a child, which made her death doubly outrageous.

It could happen to me, too, Lauren thought suddenly. She quickly banished the idea from her mind and concentrated on the girl's hair.

Ellen's short blond hair had obviously been professionally cut and carefully shaped. The ends had been softly flipped away from her face. It was simple yet chic. Appropriate for a budding artist. It had never before occurred to Lauren that one could see a person's aspirations in a hairstyle.

She looked in the bathroom mirror after Kobelski had gone. Her own hair was a medium brown. It was parted in the middle and tightly pulled back by a clasp at the nape of her neck. The ends of her hair just touched the lower part of her shoulder blades. The style was not becoming. She wondered why she had never realized that before.

It would be good to make a change.

Lauren didn't sleep well that night. She would not have been surprised by nightmares about being strangled, but instead she dreamed of Doug. He was the man she'd nearly married. Except that her ideas about continuing her education and pursuing a career and Doug's ideas of what a wife should be were diametrically opposed. They'd start talking about it and always end up quarreling. Finally, Lauren realized that she had to choose between Doug and her professional future. She had been somewhat surprised that she had no doubts about what her decision would be.

But her certainty did not lessen the heartache of breaking the engagement. Nor did it lessen her pain when, only three months later, Doug became engaged to someone else.

Her mother had offered her little consolation. "Just goes to show, all he wanted from you was what he could get from any female. You're better off without him, Laurie."

Lauren awoke depressed, the way she always felt after dreaming about Doug or her mother.

The Kincaid Institute for Medical Research was only six blocks away, but Lauren decided to take her car that morning. She had to work until four-thirty and there'd be little time to get to the bank before it closed at five. From there she could go to a hairdresser. She'd checked the yellow pages before leaving her apartment. A number of beauty salons were open on Thursday evenings. She could call one from work and make an appointment.

The Institute was housed in a cluster of tall gray modern buildings on the other side of East Hamilton Avenue. Lauren worked in Building Four which was devoted to immunological research.

She hurried up the stairs to the second floor. Ordinarily, she loved the feeling she got whenever she entered Building Four. Long austere corridors, lined with blue-gray fluorescent lights. Shiny floors, stainless steel fixtures, the odors of various chemicals in the air. She always felt a little thrill of excitement whenever she thought about the important work being done here.

But this morning her thoughts were elsewhere.

In the bright light of day, her agreement with Kobelski seemed unreal. She would easily have admitted to dreaming the whole thing except that there was five hundred dollars in her handbag.

She unlocked the door of Lab 207. Paul Bernstein, her fellow technician, wasn't in yet. She didn't expect Dr. Herbert to be in at all today. Overseeing the project in 207 was only a small part of his job.

She flicked on the fluorescent overhead lights, shoved her handbag into the bottom drawer of her desk and put on her white lab coat.

Paul came in, glowering as usual. He was a slightly built young man with dark hair and complexion. He was a moody, intense person and Lauren never knew quite what to expect from him.

"Good morning, Paul," Lauren said cheerfully.

" 'Morning," he growled, without looking up as he pulled on his lab coat.

He opened the refrigerator and began shoving racks of test tubes from one side of the shelves to the other.

"What happened to my samples?" he demanded.

"Which ones?" Lauren had no idea what he was talking about.

"The ones I was working with yesterday," he said impatiently. "The samples from Houston. The tubes had yellow tape on them. I put the rack right here in front. You must have taken them out." His face was flushed with anger.

Whenever anything went wrong, Paul's first reaction was to blame Lauren. After it had happened several times, she talked to her boss. Dr. Herbert was a stout grandfatherly man with rosy cheeks and little wisps of white hair encircling his nearly bald head.

"I know Paul's difficult to work with, my dear," he'd said gently, looking at her over the top of his rimless glasses. "But surely you realize that he's jealous of you?"

"Jealous? Why?"

"Because Paul tried to get into graduate school last semester and the semester before. He almost qualified for it both times. Sometimes a near miss is more disappointing than outright failure." Dr. Herbert had smiled kindly at her. "Do you see why he resents you?"

After that, Lauren felt a mixture of compassion and irritation toward Paul. She could understand how let down he must feel, especially if he had wanted to go to school as much as she did.

But still, it was difficult to take Paul's resentment day after day and not fight back.

Now she gritted her teeth and reminded herself that she was a professional. "I didn't take your samples, Paul." She removed a rack from the refrigerator. "These are the ones I tested last night. They're the only ones I handled."

He seized the rack and inspected the samples in it, one by one. When he had satisfied himself that they were not the ones he was looking for, he shoved the rack angrily into Lauren's hands and stalked off.

She bit her lip and waited a few moments until she had her temper under control. "Let me look for your samples, Paul. Perhaps they're right here and you just didn't notice them."

But they weren't. Lauren carefully checked all the samples in the refrigerator and none were labeled "Houston." Paul hunched over his desk in an attitude of despair.

Lauren looked around the counters in the lab, in the water baths and in the centrifuges. Finally, she opened the door of the freezer, where serum samples were stored. In the front of the center shelf was a rack of test tubes with yellow tape on them. The name "Houston" preceded the code number on each tube.

Freezing had ruined the samples, of course. Their tests were designed to be run on fresh blood. It was possible to type frozen blood, but Lab 207 wasn't equipped to do it. And even if it had been, it would be poor scientific procedure to test some samples in a different manner from the rest.

Paul stared at the rack unbelievingly. "I'm *sure* I put it in the refrigerator," he declared for the third time. There was nothing Lauren could say. She only wished she didn't have the feeling that he was blaming her.

"It's easy enough to see how it happened," she said consolingly.

"But what am I going to do?" Paul fretted. "I haven't finished testing them. What'll Dr. Herbert say?"

Lauren's impatience disappeared in a flood of pity. Paul was really as helpless as a child sometimes! And just as frightened.

"Tell you what," she offered. "I'll call Houston this

afternoon and tell them the samples were ruined accidentally. I don't have to say how. Perhaps they can send us
duplicates.''

Relief showed on Paul's face for a moment. Then his
expression hardened into one of inscrutability. "Thanks,"
he said curtly as he walked away.

Lauren suppressed an urge to scream. The ungrateful
wretch! Was that any way to act?

After work, Lauren hurried to the bank. She exchanged
one of the hundred-dollar bills for smaller bills and depos-
ited the other four hundred dollars in her checking account.
The teller, possibly used to college students who received
large amounts of money from home, didn't give her a second glance.

Lauren walked out of the bank slowly. There was no turning back now, she realized. By taking the money, she had
committed herself to going through with Kobelski's plan.

The beauty salon was a blend of chrome, glass, fluorescent lights, and pale blue fixtures. Because it was the dinner
hour, there were only a few customers. A thin, anemic-
looking girl with an elaborately styled platinum hairdo attended to her. Lauren tried not to feel self-conscious as she
described the new color and hairstyle she wanted.

"That's going to make you look really different," the girl
warned her. "You'd be better off just having it cut first and
getting used to short hair. Then you could have it lightened gradually."

"No, I want to do it all at once," Lauren insisted.

The girl looked at her doubtfully. "Well, just don't say I
didn't warn you. I've had this happen before. Some girl will
say she wants to look completely different. Then, when the
job's done, she's unhappy."

"Do it all at once," Lauren said firmly. "I promise I
won't complain."

When the girl had finished working on her, Lauren
looked in the mirror. For a dizzying moment, Ellen Rickover stared back at her.

CHAPTER THREE

The shock of not recognizing herself passed quickly, but Lauren was left with an uneasy feeling. She tried to dispel it by taking a critical look at her new appearance.

The hairstyle was flattering. Her complexion was fair, it looked natural with blond hair, and now she could see and appreciate the long, slender line of her neck. Flipping her hair back that way softened the lines of her face and made her eyes seem wider. In spite of everything else, she felt an unfamiliar sense of satisfaction. She tipped the hairdresser generously.

It was nearly nine o'clock by the time she returned to her apartment. A taxi was parked at the curb in front of the building. A small white-haired woman was standing on the sidewalk. She wore a neat navy blue coat and a small old-fashioned black hat. She was holding a birdcage and spouting commands to the cab driver, who was struggling with a large trunk at the top of the front steps. The little woman was surrounded by suitcases.

Lauren was puzzled. The lady was obviously moving in, but none of the apartments were vacant.

"Can I help you?" she asked as she approached.

"Oh, thank you!" The woman's face crinkled into a smile. "I'm Miss Emerson—Lloyd's sister. He's in the hospital having surgery and I've come to stay in his apartment. He's worried about burglars and vandals. Worries far too much, if you ask me!" She paid the driver and turned back to Lauren. "Do you live here, too?"

Lauren nodded and introduced herself. "I have the apartment across the hall. May I help you take some of these things in?"

"Oh, mercy! That would be *so* nice!" Miss Emerson fumbled in her bag for a key as she glanced around the foyer, her sharp bright eyes taking in the incongruous mix of old elegance and failing present practicality: the leaded glass window, the massive chandelier, and the cracking linoleum.

After they had carried the bags inside and maneuvered the trunk across the foyer and into the Emerson apartment, the little woman thanked Lauren. "Perhaps you'd stay for a cup of tea?" she suggested. "If I can figure out where Lloyd keeps the teabags."

Lauren smiled. "Thanks, but not this time. I'm sure you've got plenty to do right now and I really must study."

Miss Emerson's bright eyes showed interest. "Of course, dearie. What are you studying?"

"I'm working toward a degree in immunology," Lauren explained as she checked her mailbox. Besides a flyer advertising a department store sale, there was a letter from Ma.

"My, so ambitious!" Miss Emerson clucked. "In my day, a girl didn't have such opportunities. She was expected to get married and start a family. And if she couldn't catch a man, she was supposed to become a teacher or a nurse." She shrugged her thin little shoulders and laughed. "Between us, it's a lot better this way!"

The letter from Ma was almost standard. She wrote faithfully every week, always on notepaper with little flowers at the top of the page, and each letter said practically the same thing.

> *Dear Lauren,*
> *How are you?*
> *I don't think I'll ever get used to this hot weather. I don't know how people lived here before they had air conditioning.*
> *Yesterday I applied for a job as an aide in a nursing home.*

That sentence always varied somewhat. Last week she'd

applied for a job as a clerk in a souvenir shop. The week before, as a saleslady in a bakery.

I hope I find a job soon. There are so few openings and so many people apply for each one.
Hope you are fine and doing well in school.
        Love,
        Ma

Lauren's heart ached as she put the letter down. If only she and Ma could really talk to each other. She sighed. It had never been that way and it never would be.

As was her habit, she sat down and immediately answered her mother's letter.

Dear Ma and Aunt Lil,

That was pure diplomacy. Aunt Lil never wrote to her.

It was good to get your letter.
The weather here is beautiful. The trees are in full color.
School is fine. I think I can get A's in both of my courses.
I hope that the job at the nursing home comes through.

Lauren stopped and read what she had written. Her letters all sounded alike, too. What else could she say? She certainly couldn't tell them about the deal she'd made with Kobelski!

I had my hair cut short today.

She hesitated. She would not mention having had her hair lightened as well. Ma and Aunt Lil still clung to the notion that any woman who bleached her hair was a "hussy."

It looks nicer and will be easier to care for.
I hope you're both feeling well.
        Love,
        Lauren

She reread her words with dissatisfaction. Talk about superficial communication! With a sigh, she folded the letter and inserted it into an envelope.

Lauren found it difficult to concentrate on cytology that night. The illustrations of tissue cells suddenly all looked alike.

Kobelski hadn't told her when he'd be back. And when she had asked how she could contact him, he said, "You don't. I'll keep in touch." She would have to wait and see what happened.

It was nearly eleven by the time she had covered the material for the next morning's class. She decided to take a hot shower. It had been a long day, and her muscles were cramped from tension. She hoped the steamy shower would help her relax so that she would sleep better than she had last night.

The bathroom was small and windowless. It had been tucked into a corner off the kitchenette to simplify the plumbing when the one-family house was converted into apartments. It wasn't the best of floor plans. She had to cross the living room to go from her bedroom to the bathroom. But, since she lived alone, it didn't really matter.

Lauren pulled all the shades and laid her nightgown on the bed. No sense in getting it all steamed up and damp. She carefully adjusted her shower cap to protect her hair.

The hot water pounding on her back felt good. Tension drained away from her body. She lathered herself from head to toe and let the water rinse the lather away. Feeling considerably better, she wrapped herself in a large towel and stepped out of the bathroom in a cloud of steam. The cooler air of the apartment felt good, too.

"Take it off."

Startled by the voice, Lauren turned to see Kobelski lounging on the sofa. His hands were clasped behind his head, and his feet were resting on the little yellow table.

"Take it off," he commanded again.

Lauren was too frightened to react. "Wh-what?"

"The shower cap. Take it off. I want to see how your hair looks."

Still a bit stunned, Lauren plucked the cap off and shook

her head to let her hair fall into place.

Kobelski smiled. "Very nice."

His gaze traveled downward and Lauren felt a sudden surge of fury. She pulled the towel closer around herself. "What in hell are you doing here, Kobelski?" she demanded.

He seemed amused by her anger. "Why don't you get dressed?" he suggested, leaning farther back into the sofa. "Then we can talk."

Lauren's hands were shaking with indignation as she pulled a pair of jeans and a cotton shirt out of her bedroom closet.

Who did he think he was, walking into her apartment like that? What gave him the right—— She stopped.

The door had been locked. She always kept her door locked. A girl living alone couldn't take chances. And she had checked the door again when she pulled the shades just before taking her shower.

Her fingers trembled so that she could scarcely button the front of her shirt. Fear and anger battled within her. Anger won.

She was going to give Kobelski a piece of her mind! His invasion of her privacy was an outrage!

But he stood up when she returned to the living room, and it gave him a psychological advantage. With his huge frame towering over her, angry words suddenly seemed useless.

"How did you get in?" she asked lamely. "I know the door was locked."

He shrugged. "In my business, you get to know a lot about locks. And the first thing you learn is that they don't stop anybody who really wants to get in."

Lauren sat down in the faded green easy chair which had once belonged to her grandmother. Kobelski dropped back onto the sofa. He wore a freshly pressed suit tonight. And a tie, though it was loosened. Despite her anger with him, Lauren thought he looked quite handsome.

"Why didn't you knock? I would have let you in."

Kobelski gave her a long look. "I *did* knock. But then I heard the water pipes rattling, so I knew you were in the shower and couldn't hear me."

"You *could* have waited in the hall," she reminded him icily.

"Uh-uh." His manner was that of an adult explaining to a child. "I've been asking a lot of questions in this town. Too many people know I'm a detective. If I'm seen hanging around you, how effective a bait do you think you'd be?"

It sounded logical enough.

"Just the same," she said, "I don't like your coming into my apartment anytime you feel like it. If you want me to go along with this deal, you've got to promise that you won't come here uninvited anymore."

He seemed amused by her attitude, but he nodded. "Okay. Anything to keep you happy."

He pulled out several snapshots from his wallet. "More pictures. Take a look at them and get an idea of the way the girls dressed."

Lauren looked the snapshots over carefully. Most of them were of Ellen Rickover. There were only three of Diane Towle. Diane obviously liked to dress up, while Ellen preferred to dress down. Both, however, had excellent taste. And, if she could judge from the snapshots, both spent a small fortune on their wardrobes.

Nothing in her own closet even came close. Lauren lived mostly in jeans and cotton shirts. It was typical campus dress. And she had never thought of dressing up to work in the lab, where she might spill blood samples or chemicals on anything that wasn't covered by her lab coat.

"Again," Kobelski said, "I suggest that you buy a few outfits similar to the Rickover girl's. Her tastes suit your personality better."

Lauren was annoyed. "How would you know?"

He just grinned, which annoyed her even more.

Lauren found Ellen's wardrobe inviting. Casual shirts, well-cut slacks and pantsuits, a gracefully flowing caftan.

They were clothes she'd love to wear. It was going to be fun shopping for them.

Kobelski leaned forward. "You'd better wear more makeup, too. Emphasize your eyes. Both girls had long, dark lashes."

She nodded. "Okay. And I'll go shopping on Saturday for the clothes."

He reached for his wallet. "Need more money?"

"Not yet. But I'll be sure to let you know when I do. Any other instructions?"

"Just don't discourage any man who shows an interest in you. But don't lead him on either. If you get too aggressive, it might scare him off."

"Got you, chief!" She grinned. She was getting giddy. Right now, it was hard to believe there was any danger in this. It was a game, a big joke they were going to play on some unsuspecting stranger. "Like some coffee?" she asked.

"Sounds good. I've got a long night ahead."

She got up and turned toward the tiny kitchenette.

"Don't do that!"

Lauren whirled around to look at him. Kobelski stood up and gave her a fierce look. The scar on his left cheek stood out in a ragged white line.

"What's wrong?" she asked, frightened.

"You turned your back on me!" His teeth were clenched in anger. "I warned you not to do that!"

Lauren felt dizzy. "But you—I—I can trust *you!*"

His expression was still grim. "This is no game, Lauren! From now on, you trust *no one*."

"But I *have* to trust *you!*"

Kobelski sighed and rubbed his chin. "Maybe I was wrong. I shouldn't have gotten you into this." He stared at her for a long moment.

Lauren felt confused. "You're either crazy or terribly inconsistent," she said slowly. "When I was upset that you had broken into my apartment, you seemed to think that I shouldn't have been alarmed at all. Now you're getting hot about a much smaller thing!''

Kobelski shook his head and put up a hand as if to silence her. ''When you found me here, you were angry and frightened. Your guard was up. That was good.''

He paused as if to make sure she was listening. ''But a moment ago, you let your guard down. That's bad. Next time, it could cost you your life.''

Lauren felt suddenly weak.

''Better sit down,'' he said softly. ''You don't look so good.'' He took her arm and led her back to the chair. ''You all right?''

She nodded. ''You just scared the hell out of me, that's all.''

A slow grin spread across his face. ''Good! Then you'll remember what I said.''

''You're *mean*, Kobelski! Did you know that?''

He gave her a searching look. ''Having second thoughts?''

''Yes! Lots of them!'' she said angrily. ''But I'm not quitting! You haven't scared me off!''

She saw in his eyes that he was pleased. Then she understood. ''You've been testing my nerve, haven't you?''

He just smiled.

He motioned for her to stay where she was. ''Tell me where everything is,'' he said. ''I'll make the coffee.''

CHAPTER FOUR

"You make good coffee." She sipped the steaming liquid from the stoneware mug that Kobelski had handed her.

"Thanks. I'm a pretty good cook, too. Comes from living alone." He settled back down on the sofa, and Lauren couldn't help noticing that his hands were so large that one of them almost completely encircled his coffee mug.

"Tell me about yourself," he said softly.

"I thought you already knew everything."

That brought a smile. "Not *everything*. Just the available facts."

"What do you want to know?"

"What makes you tick."

"I'm not sure how to answer that," she said slowly. "I've always wanted to be *somebody*. That's all. To me, that means knowing a lot."

He nodded as if he understood perfectly.

"I suppose a psychiatrist would say I'm trying to win approval in order to compensate for my father's rejection of me."

"Do you remember him at all?"

She remembered being suddenly plucked from the floor and tossed into the air. She'd giggled with delight. Two strong arms had caught her and hugged her against a woolen jacket which smelled faintly of dampness and pipe tobacco. Her father had had dark wavy hair and a deep throaty chuckle. She remembered the after-shave lotion he'd worn, too. It was an unusual scent. Bittersweet. A foreign brand, probably. From time to time, she met men who used the same after-shave—she'd never had the nerve to ask the

27

name of it—and always the scent awakened a sharp sense of pain within her.

"I remember only good things," she said slowly. "I never did understand why he left us. My mother's version is obviously biased."

"She took it hard?"

"She tried to kill herself." Her voice wavered. She looked up at him and added quickly, "But it's—it's hard to judge how serious she was. You see, she swallowed a lot of sleeping pills and immediately called the doctor."

"Was that the only time?"

His voice was gentle but insistent. Lauren felt painful memories assailing her. Her first impulse was to tell Kobelski to mind his own business, but his manner was so clearly sympathetic that she couldn't do it.

"No, it wasn't. She tried again when I was nine. She— I'm not exactly sure what happened. No one really told me. From what I overheard, she ran into my father somewhere. That was shortly after Gram had died, and I guess it was just too much." She paused and swallowed. "And, of course, she tried again when I told her I was leaving home to go to graduate school."

"Of course?"

"Well, you can understand—I mean, my father left her and now *I* was leaving. To her it seemed like the same thing."

"And yet, you *did* leave." It was a statement. He wasn't accusing her, and Lauren was grateful.

"I *had* to. Once it occurred to her that I might really leave, she became impossible to live with. I couldn't go out of the house without letting her know where I was going. She was constantly checking on me. She'd get upset if I came home ten minutes late."

Kobelski nodded. "Did she react that badly when you were going to get married?"

"You know about *that*, too?"

He shrugged. "It's an available fact. Your engagement announcement was in the newspapers."

"You're a stickler for detail, aren't you?"

He shrugged again. "I'm efficient. How did she react?"

"Not that badly." Lauren smiled. "Of course, it never occurred to me at the time, but she probably assumed she'd live with us. Or at least next door."

"She needs psychiatric treatment, you know."

"Oh, I tried that, too. It took a lot of persuasion to get her to a psychiatrist, and she quit after the first visit."

"Why?"

"She said he asked too many personal questions." Lauren sighed. "You see how it was. There was nothing more I could do. Finally, I wrote to Aunt Lil in Florida and asked her whether Mother could stay with her for a while."

"And she agreed."

"I was pretty sure she would. She's always been protective of my mother. Aunt Lil never approved of my father. All she said when he left was, 'I told you so.'

"She never liked me much, either—I suppose because of my father. Now she thinks I'm an ungrateful daughter who doesn't know where her responsibilities lie."

Kobelski rubbed his chin thoughtfully. "You feel guilty?"

Lauren nodded. "But I try not to. I know I did everything I could, short of letting her drive me crazy. I *had* to leave."

"Took guts, though."

"Thanks. It's nice to know someone understands."

"Did you love him?" he asked abruptly.

"What?" Lauren looked at him. "Who?"

"The guy you almost married."

"Oh! Doug." She hesitated. "Do you really think that's any of your business?"

He shrugged. "It could be."

"I don't see how."

He didn't reply and, oddly enough, his silence made her feel obliged to answer. "Well, of course I loved him. I wouldn't have considered marrying him if I didn't love him."

"But you changed your mind."

"It would have been a mistake." Her voice was brittle. "We had different sets of values. Different goals."

"I see."

"Is that good or bad?"

He smiled. "Mostly good."

"Why?"

"It shows that you tend to make your decisions logically instead of emotionally."

"Oh!"

They sat for a moment in silence.

"What's your first name?" Lauren asked.

A faint color came to Kobelski's face. He hesitated. "Ernest," he said quietly.

"Ernest. Ernie." She looked at him. "It doesn't fit you."

He grinned approvingly. "I never thought so, either." Then he sobered and stared at her.

"What are you thinking about?" she asked.

"About what you said. That you wanted to be somebody."

"So?"

"Ellen and Diane both wanted to be somebody."

Lauren shivered. "I'm like them in that way, too, aren't I?"

"There are a lot of similarities." He set down his empty mug and searched through the photos until he found a close-up of each girl. He laid the pictures side by side on the table and stared at them.

Lauren noticed that the picture of Ellen Rickover was considerably worn. The edges had been tattered as if someone had carried the photo around for a long time. Kobelski must have gotten it from Ellen's parents, she thought. It must have been painful for them to part with it.

"So many similarities," Kobelski said again. "If only we knew which ones trigger this guy."

Lauren suddenly realized her hands were cold and she rubbed them together. "What do *you* think?"

He shook his head. "There's no way to tell. He's obviously attracted to a certain physical type. But that isn't necessarily why he kills.''

"Explain that a little more. I'm not sure I understand."

"I think he's an obsessive-compulsive. Know what that means?"

She nodded. "He has an overwhelming urge to do certain things, and may not even know why."

"Right. He may be killing these girls simply because they look like someone he hates. Maybe his mother. Maybe an old girlfriend."

"Or a wife?"

"Perhaps."

"You said it was possible that it isn't just the physical appearance."

Kobelski nodded. "He may be drawn to her by her looks and triggered to kill by something else."

"For instance?"

"Suppose he figures she doesn't pay enough attention to him. She's too involved with her ambitions."

"Because she wants to be somebody?" Horrified at her own words, Lauren covered her mouth with her hand.

"You said it, not I."

"Damn it, Kobelski! You really know how to scare a girl!"

"Sorry," he said soberly. "But you have to understand these things. I'm relying on you to size up any fellow you run into. Psychologically, I mean."

"I don't know anything about psychology."

"You seem to have sized up your mother pretty well. And it's not easy when you're that close to someone."

Lauren's eyes widened. "I see now that there's a purpose in every question you ask." As she often did when she was uncomfortable, Lauren attempted a little humor. "And I thought you were interested in *me!*" she teased.

"Oh, but I am!" His eyes twinkled as he looked directly into hers. Then he got up and took the two coffee mugs to the sink and carefully rinsed them.

Lauren stared at her hands. "This—this fellow—the

killer. Is there anything that will help me to know who he is?''

He shook his head. "He's certainly out of his mind when he kills, of course. But he probably appears to be perfectly normal. You'd be surprised how sane a psychotic person can seem to be." He gave her a long look. "Everything depends on your instincts. They'd better be good."

CHAPTER FIVE

Lauren was just finishing a glass of orange juice when she heard a timid knock on the door.

"Who is it?"

"Miss Emerson, dearie. I hope I'm not waking you."

Lauren opened the door. The little woman was wrapped in a thick lavender robe which could not conceal the high neck of an old-fashioned nightgown.

"I'm so sorry to bother you at this hour," Miss Emerson said brightly, holding out an empty teacup. "But I wonder whether I could borrow a little milk. Lloyd doesn't seem to have any, and I simply can't stand black coffee in the morning."

"No trouble at all," Lauren said cheerfully. "Come on in."

As she took the milk pitcher from the refrigerator, she noticed that Miss Emerson was inspecting the apartment. *I'll bet she doesn't miss a thing*, Lauren thought, amused.

The woman poked a forefinger into the soil of one of the plants on the windowsill. "This coleus needs repotting, dearie. It's definitely rootbound."

"I know." Lauren sighed as she filled the cup with milk. "Several of my plants should be repotted. I'm afraid I've neglected them lately."

"Oh, I understand. You're such a busy young woman. Between working and going to school——" Miss Emerson paused as if struck by a wonderful idea. "Why don't you let me repot them for you? I'd be glad for something to do during the day."

"That's sweet of you, but I really couldn't let——"

"Nonsense! Of course, you can let me. Indulge an old

woman, dearie. I love plants." Her uptilted chin told Lauren that it would do no good to refuse.

"Well, if you really want to. But I don't have any empty pots."

"No problem. I have plenty at home. My nephew is coming by this afternoon to bring me some groceries. I'll ask him to drop by my house and pick up some pots."

There was no arguing with Miss Emerson once she had made up her mind. She flitted from one plant to another. "This one, too. And this one. And I'll cut them back a little, as well. It revitalizes them, you know."

Lauren smiled.

Miss Emerson finally chose eight plants that needed immediate tending, and Lauren helped her carry them into the apartment across the hall. Once, as they were going back and forth, Lauren saw Miss Emerson's gaze rest briefly on the two coffee mugs standing near the sink.

I wonder what she makes of that? Lauren thought. *I'll have to warn Kobelski to be extra careful if he doesn't want anyone to know he's around. There's not much she misses."*

The morning promised a clear Indian summer day. The air was brisk and the leaves, at the height of their color, were just beginning to fall. Lauren drove across town to the university. On Mondays, Wednesdays, and Fridays, Lauren attended classes in the morning and worked from one o'clock until nine at night.

She parked her car in Area 17, the main campus parking lot. It was a sea of cars and the university, short on funds in all departments, couldn't afford much security. Lauren had been warned when she applied for a parking permit that Area 17 was a popular target of car thieves. Most of them were teenagers who took cars for a lark. The stolen cars were usually recovered after a day or two. But some of them were badly damaged, and others were never seen again.

Lauren's secondhand Ford was twelve years old, but its

former owner had driven it carefully and kept it in top condition. If it were stolen, Lauren knew it would be impossible to replace it for the money she'd receive from the insurance company. On the advice of a service station mechanic, she had had a gasoline cutoff switch installed beneath the dashboard. With a flick of her toe, the gas was prevented from entering the carburetor.

"It won't stop anybody who really wants to steal the car," the mechanic had warned. "They'd find the switch after a couple of minutes of poking around. But these kids don't care which car they take, and if your car won't start right away, they're far more likely to take a different one instead of trying to figure out how to start yours."

Lauren used the cutoff switch faithfully whenever she left her car in Area 17, although she seldom thought of it at other times.

Lauren loved the campus. It sprawled at the edge of the city and bordered a medium-sized lake. Curving tree-lined walks connected the various buildings, whose ages were proclaimed by their architectural style. Fulton Hall, built in 1857 with graceful Greek columns and a precisely angled roof, had once dominated the gently rolling hills. It had even managed to subdue the later buildings, those vast outcroppings of brick and stone which had been designed more for practicality than for visual effect.

Now, however, the new Life Sciences Building, a fifteen-story structure of steel and glass, towered over once-proud Fulton Hall, reducing it to an anachronism.

Lauren's nine o'clock class was a cytology lecture. The class was small, only twenty students. About half of them attended the two-hour laboratory session which followed.

As she took her seat in the lecture hall, Lauren realized that she was attracting attention.

Is it only the change, or do they see the resemblance?

"What have you done to yourself?" Nedra Hines, a small dark girl with a rather prominent nose, sat down next to her.

"Do you like it?" Lauren asked.

"Love it! But you really do look different!" Nedra squinted at her. "What brought this on? Have you found someone interesting?"

Lauren shrugged. "Uh-uh. I just felt like a change." She wondered whether her voice sounded as casual as she hoped.

Professor Warren Bell taught Lauren's cytology course. He was a lean athletic man in his early forties, whose handsome craggy features were set off by his modishly styled blond hair and a deep golden tan. He had a reputation for eccentricity, probably because he dressed and often acted as though he were half his age.

"He prefers women half his age, too," Nedra had told her during the first week of classes. "Of course, he's goodlooking, and there are plenty of girls who don't mind going out with a man who's old enough to be their father. But once in a while he sets his sights on a girl who doesn't feel that way. If that should happen to you, play *dumb!*" she had advised. "Act as if you don't understand. Because if you come right out and refuse, he'll be offended and your grades might take a nose dive."

"He can't do that!" Lauren had protested.

"Oh, yes, he can! His sister's married to the dean. And what Warren Bell wants, he gets."

At first, Lauren was inclined to think that Nedra was exaggerating. Professor Bell's academic reputation was beyond question. He had written several well-known books, including the texts used in both of Lauren's cytology courses. He obviously loved his subject, and his enthusiasm electrified his classes. Lauren admired him tremendously as a teacher.

And yet, she noticed that every time Professor Bell spoke to one of his female students, he somehow managed to hold her hand or brush her hair out of her eyes. And in the laboratory he was constantly helping the girls set up their equipment, guiding their hands as they prepared slides and adjusted microscopes.

The buzz of students' voices died down as Professor Bell

entered the room and mounted the podium. Today he wore tailored jeans and an embroidered peasant shirt. He shuffled through his notes and glanced around the room. His gaze fell on Lauren and remained there for a moment. She felt her cheeks grow hot and wondered whether Nedra was right after all. She bent over her notebook and pretended to be having trouble getting her pen to work.

After a moment, Bell cleared his throat and began the morning's lecture. "Today we'll discuss the protein structure of ribosomes and their functions within the cell."

As always, Lauren took careful notes. Bell's material was thoroughly organized and brilliantly presented. He made full use of slides and vividly colored illustrations, and he often used lighting effects or special demonstrations to make a particular point unforgettable.

Afterward, on their way to the laboratory session, Nedra hurried alongside of Lauren, puffing as they mounted the stairs.

"Boy, going blond really gets results! All the guys are staring at you!"

Lauren was uncomfortably aware of the fact. *I should be enjoying this,* she thought. *Instead I'm wondering whether one of them is going to try to kill me!*

Aloud, she said, "I guess I'll have to get used to it."

"That shouldn't be too hard to do," Nedra murmured enviously.

In the cytology lab, Lauren checked the Petrie dishes containing the bacterial cultures she had prepared earlier in the week. They had come along nicely and she could begin to prepare slides from them today.

She arranged her materials carefully. Clean glass plates, cover slips, a little rack with various staining solutions, clean pipettes. It was precise work, requiring skillful fingers and a good deal of patience, but Lauren enjoyed making slides. There was a great satisfaction in taking a drop of cloudy-looking fluid and transforming it into a clearly defined specimen. Carefully, she placed a cover slip on the slide she had finished.

"Miss Walker?" Professor Bell was standing beside her. "Could we meet in my office after class today? I'd like a conference with you."

"A conference? What about?" Lauren frowned. "Isn't my work satisfactory?"

Bell smiled warmly at her. "Yes, quite. That is, except for your last quiz." He put his hand lightly on her arm. "It wasn't up to your usual high standards."

Lauren stared at him in surprise. She hadn't thought she'd had any problems with that quiz. They'd been shown slides of various types of tissue and asked to identify them. Lauren had recognized each one. And she'd been able to identify the components of the cells when the slides had been magnified. She couldn't believe that she'd done badly.

Bell rested one hip on the edge of her desk. "Well, can you meet with me?"

"I—not today." Lauren looked at the clock. "I have to go to work."

"Ah, yes. You *are* only a part-time student, aren't you? I can understand how difficult it is for you to keep up."

She looked at him sharply. Was that concern or condescension? His pale blue eyes gave her no hint of his thoughts.

"Can't you tell me what was wrong with my work?" she asked.

He toyed with the massive oriental ring he wore. "I would much prefer to sit down with you and look the paper over. We need to discuss it thoroughly." He paused and waited.

Lauren said nothing.

"Saturday morning, perhaps?" he prompted.

There was no way out of it. "Okay," she agreed. There was a sinking feeling in her stomach. If Nedra was right about Bell, she—Lauren—was in for trouble, and her grades for the semester might be in jeopardy. And if Nedra was wrong, and Bell was on the level, and she really had done badly on the quiz, her grades still might be in jeopardy. What a rotten time for this to happen!

"What time would you like me to come?" she asked.

The merest suggestion of a smile played across his lips. "Eleven-thirty all right?"

As Lauren was putting away her things, Nedra came up to her. "I hate to say 'I told you so,' but I did, didn't I? What did he want?"

Lauren sighed. "A *conference*. He says I fouled up the last quiz, and I don't think I did!"

Nedra gave her a significant look. "You're in for it! I think he's selected you for his next conquest. That conference is going to be a thinly veiled blackmail session."

"He can't do that," Lauren said angrily. "There are laws, aren't there?"

"Oh, sure, there are laws. But what are you going to say in court? Bell's pretty shifty. He never comes right out and *says* anything. It's all implied. And if he flunks you, what judge is going to be able to decide how much you know about cytology? That's Bell's word against yours, and he's the professor!"

CHAPTER SIX

Lauren, leaving the Life Sciences Building, felt very discouraged. What good would Thomas Rickover's money do her if she flunked out of school? But she certainly wasn't going to sell herself for a grade! She had to think of a way to handle Professor Bell without endangering her scholastic standing.

As she turned a corner on her way to the Student Union, she collided with a sandy-haired young man wearing jeans and a sweatshirt that proclaimed, "Kiss me, I'm Irish!" Her books and papers went flying.

"Oh, hey, I'm sorry!" He bent to pick up her things.

"My fault," Lauren murmured. "I wasn't looking where I was going."

"You should have been," he chided her. "I might have been a Mack truck. And wouldn't that have put a crimp in your day?"

She laughed. He was good-looking and clean-cut, with a trim athletic build. His smile was as friendly as a puppy's. He handed her things to her.

"You don't look Irish." Lauren pointed to his shirt.

"I'm not. But don't let that stop you." He held out his arms and his eyes twinkled with amusement.

Lauren felt her cheeks grow hot as she stared at the sidewalk. She'd walked right into that one! How stupid of her!

"Hey! Don't be embarrassed," he said kindly. "I don't usually kiss on the first collision, either."

She couldn't help smiling.

"Stay happy," he said with a wink as he left. "It becomes you."

41

She watched him saunter down the hill whistling a cheerful tune and realized that her spirits were considerably higher than they had been a short while before. "Thanks, whoever you are," she murmured to herself. "I needed that!"

After a quick lunch in the union cafeteria, she checked her watch. If she drove straight back to her apartment, she could walk the six blocks to work. Soon the weather would turn cold, and a day like this was too precious not to enjoy. Besides, the exercise would do her good.

"Good afternoon, Paul," she said brightly as she entered the lab.

" 'Afternoon," he muttered. Then he turned to look at her and started. "You—what have you done? You look so—different!"

"I just had my hair done," Lauren said lightly. "No big deal."

Paul wouldn't let it go, however. "But why?" he asked suspiciously. "And why did you do it now? You must have a reason!"

She was surprised. She hadn't expected him to react at all, much less like this! "Oh, Paul! Haven't you ever done anything on impulse? Without a reason?"

"Yes, but——" He clenched his fists and Lauren watched his knuckles grow white.

"But what?" she insisted.

"They were always things I shouldn't have done," he mumbled as he bent over his test tubes.

Lauren always spent her Fridays at the lab summarizing the results of the week's testing. The project that she and Paul worked on was Dr. Herbert's pet and was quite simple in its design. Each week, samples of blood from patients in hospitals all over the country were sent to 207. Lauren and Paul tested them for more than a hundred factors, including antigens, enzymes, and various proteins. The results of the testing were then fed into computers along with the medical histories of the patients from whom the samples had come.

Dr. Herbert believed that there was a definite correlation between a person's blood chemistry and the diseases he was prone to. Some of these correlations had already been discovered. Duodenal ulcers, for example, occurred most frequently in persons whose blood type was O. Dr. Herbert was dedicated to finding more such correlations.

As she transcribed her test results onto the data sheets from which the computer cards would be punched, Lauren could feel that Paul was watching her. But every time she glanced up, he quickly went back to his work. It made her uncomfortable, and she had to force herself to concentrate on her work. Before long she had a headache.

At about four o'clock, Dr. Herbert came in to check their progress. Lauren always felt a little anxious when he was examining her work. His mind was razor-sharp, and his tongue, too, despite his grandfatherly appearance. He had little patience with those who were unable to grasp an idea as quickly as he did. Lauren dreaded the possibility that he might one day discover a serious mistake in her work.

"Good afternoon, good afternoon," Dr. Herbert greeted them cheerfully. Turning to Lauren, he added, "My word, you look pretty, my dear."

Paul glowered. Lauren knew it annoyed him to have Dr. Herbert address her as 'my dear.' No doubt Paul understood it to mean that Lauren was the favored one.

As usual, because Lauren worked late on Fridays, Dr. Herbert checked Paul's work first. Lauren hunched over her data sheets, trying not to listen, but she couldn't help overhearing the exasperation in Dr. Herbert's voice. Paul's tone was very defensive. He must have done something wrong. Dr. Herbert was really dressing him down.

She couldn't help feeling sorry for Paul. To Dr. Herbert, sloppy scientific work was unforgivable. His voice grew louder. "Careless imbecile! For such work, you expect to be paid? Bah!"

Lauren couldn't make out Paul's mumbled reply. She turned back to her data sheets. Suddenly Paul was standing up. He ripped off his lab coat and flung it angrily onto one of the large centrifuges. His face was flushed and his eyes bright as he walked over to Lauren's desk.

"I'm leaving," he said as he pulled on his rumpled sport jacket. "Have a nice weekend." Almost as an afterthought, he added sarcastically, "It's nice that Dr. Herbert likes your new look, isn't it? Is that part of the plan?"

Lauren watched openmouthed as Paul left the lab. Was that what had been bothering him all afternoon? Did he think she was playing up to the boss? Was he so paranoid that he had to find an ulterior motive in everything she did?

Dr. Herbert came over to her. "And now let's see what you've been doing this week!"

Lauren produced her notebook and data sheets. Dr. Herbert nodded as he ran his stubby finger back and forth across the pages.

"Very nice work, my dear. At least I have one competent technician!"

"I take it Paul had a problem?"

He peered at her over his glasses and snorted. "Problem! He *is* the problem! He used to be a fairly good worker. But lately! I don't believe his mind is on his work at all." He sighed and mopped his forehead with his handkerchief. "He had twenty blood tests attached to the wrong medical histories! That could have ruined the entire project! If we have the wrong correlations, we draw the wrong conclusions! And the worst part is, I don't believe Paul understands the seriousness of his mistake!"

"Maybe he's had a bad week," Lauren suggested mildly. "Perhaps after the weekend—and a little rest—he'll do better."

Dr. Herbert shook his head. "I'm afraid that rest won't help him. Something has disturbed him recently, and his work has been getting steadily worse ever since. What he needs is psychiatric help."

After Dr. Herbert left, Lauren thought about Kobelski. *He's going to be delighted. So far his bait has attracted a lecherous professor and repelled a paranoid research technician! How ironic!* She couldn't help smiling.

CHAPTER SEVEN

Lauren looked at the clock on the laboratory wall. Ten after nine. She decided to call it a day. Carefully, she placed her data sheets in sequence, checking each page to make certain it was dated and correctly identified. She put them in a neat stack on one side of her desk. Then she filed the medical histories and returned her workbook with her test results to its proper place on the shelf. Everything was in order.

She glanced around the lab with a feeling that was close to love. She liked the stainless steel sinks, the cabinets full of glassware, the shelves stocked with chemicals. Even the refrigerator containing the blood samples seemed beautiful. The lab was a small hidden window through which she could see facets of truth that most people weren't aware of. And might *never* be aware of.

There was only one thing wrong. She looked back to her desk and the data lying on it. Numbers and symbols on paper. That's all it was now. But soon the data would be fed into a computer and, perhaps, fascinating new truths would emerge. And it would be Dr. Herbert who would discover them. She would learn of them only secondhand.

Someday that would change, she vowed. Someday she would direct research and be the first to see the results. She would no longer be the number gatherer.

She glanced around the lab to make sure there was no electrical equipment that needed to be turned off, no samples or reagents left unrefrigerated.

Paul had left a half-empty cup of coffee standing on the workbench. She emptied the coffee into the sink and rinsed out the cup. Then she flicked out the overhead lights and locked the door of the lab.

As she left the building, a figure stepped out of the shadows and came toward her.

"Paul! What are you doing here at this hour?"

"I've got to talk to you. Please!"

In the light streaming from one of the ground-floor windows, Lauren could see that he was agitated. His eyes were dilated and bright. Perspiration dotted his brow.

"Okay," she said in what she hoped was a soothing tone. "Why don't you walk me home?"

They crossed East Hamilton Avenue and walked past the darkened windows of little shops closed for the night. Here and there lonely neon signs flickered their messages to passing traffic.

Paul said nothing. He appeared to be struggling to find the right words.

"What's the matter?" Lauren asked finally.

"I want you to talk to Dr. Herbert for me," he said anxiously. "I think he's going to fire me."

"Why should he do that?"

"You know why! He's got it in for me! He's been looking for an excuse to get rid of me, and now he thinks he's got one."

"What are you talking about?"

"This afternoon! I made a little mistake. Nothing much, really. I just copied some numbers onto the wrong line. He acted as though I was trying to destroy the whole project! You must have heard him!"

Lauren didn't want Paul to know that Dr. Herbert had told her what Paul had done. And she didn't want him to think that she had been listening while Dr. Herbert was reprimanding him. They turned off East Hamilton, and she was glad for the darker residential street. Paul couldn't see her face clearly as she answered, "I'm afraid I was pretty engrossed with my work this afternoon. Was he really angry?"

Paul nodded dejectedly. "He hates me!"

"Oh, I wouldn't take it so seriously." She tried to make her voice light. "Dr. Herbert's bark is far worse than his bite. He calms down just as fast as he gets worked up. And you know how he feels about this project. It's very important to him.''

"Too important! He was irrational! Just because I copied some numbers onto the wrong line!''

"Well, that could cause problems. It might throw all the results off——''

"Don't you start on me!'' He whirled to face her and grabbed her arm. Lauren was suddenly frightened. The street was deserted. Kobelski was supposed to be nearby, but was he? She hadn't seen anybody since they turned off East Hamilton.

"Take it easy, Paul,'' she said gently. "I'm your friend.''

"You did help me before,'' he acknowledged.

"Yes. And I want to help you now.''

He gave her an agonized look. "Then why did you change? Who told you to? What do they want?''

Suddenly Paul's conversation wasn't making any sense at all! "No one told me to,'' she said flatly. She felt self-conscious lying to him. But she couldn't possibly tell him the truth. "This is just a popular hairstyle right now.''

"Really?'' He brightened.

"Of course,'' she said easily, hoping she'd gotten him away from any idea of a conspiracy.

"I want to trust you.''

"You can.''

"Then you'll talk to him?''

"Sure.''

He relaxed and released her arm, and they continued walking.

Poor Paul! She always thought of him as "Poor Paul.''

"What would you like me to say to Dr. Herbert?'' she asked.

He thought a moment. "Just that—that it's unfair to make a big deal out of one mistake.'' He seemed calmer now. "I probably would have caught it anyhow.''

Lauren doubted that, but she kept silent.

"Tell him that he—he leaves no margin for error. He jumps on me for every little thing."

What he said wasn't true, Lauren realized. She knew that Dr. Herbert had overlooked a number of minor mistakes that Paul had made. It was the fundamental errors that had made him so angry.

They were in sight of her apartment building.

"I'll do what I can, Paul."

"Thanks." A note of elation came into his voice. "It will be all right, then. He'll listen to you. He'll do anything for you."

"That's not true," Lauren said carefully. "And it's not fair for you to say that."

His good mood vanished as quickly as it had come and was replaced by contempt. "Don't give me that good little girl routine! I know what you are!"

Lauren bristled. "And what exactly am I?"

"You're like all women," he said scornfully. "You use men. Wrap them around your little finger and make them do whatever you want!"

"Paul! Dr. Herbert's old enough to be my grandfather! He's simply a kind——"

"Kind! Well, he certainly chooses whom he'll be kind to! He lets you work odd hours so you can go to school, but me——Don't tell me he thinks of you as a granddaughter!"

They had reached the steps of her apartment building and she turned to face him. "You've insulted me, Paul," she said evenly. "I want an apology."

He glared at her defiantly.

When it became obvious that he wasn't going to retract his words, she went into the building. To her dismay, he followed her into the dimly lit foyer.

Now what? If she unlocked her door, would he follow her into the apartment, too?

She stood with her back to her door. "What do you want now?"

"Does this mean that you won't talk to Dr. Herbert for me?" he asked earnestly.

She stifled the impulse to laugh. "You're crazy!" She had spoken without thinking and regretted the words as soon as she had spoken them.

"Don't say that!" He flushed and his face was contorted with anger. Although the foyer was quite cool, he began perspiring again. Little rivulets trickled down the sides of his face.

For the first time, Lauren seriously considered the possibility that Paul might be dangerous. "I'm sorry——"

"Don't *ever* say that again!" He was standing very stiffly, she thought. As if he were trying hard to control himself. She noticed that his hands, dropped to his sides, were clenching and unclenching.

"I'm sorry," she repeated.

"I don't like it when people say things about me," he went on in a rising voice. "Bad things. Things that aren't true!" He stopped and stared at Lauren, who was flattening herself against the door.

She could scream, she thought. And Kobelski could get her out of this. But then they wouldn't have anything on Paul. She decided not to scream unless he tried to hurt her.

She glanced around the foyer. There was a fire ax in the alarm box. The sight of the ax made her uncomfortable and she quickly looked away from it lest Paul notice it, too.

"I don't like it——"

Abruptly, the door across the hall opened and Miss Emerson appeared with a look of disapproval on her face. Her eyes blazed and her little chin was held high.

"Young man, do you realize the disturbance you're creating?"

Paul became flustered. "I'm sorry. I didn't mean——"

"You'd better go," Miss Emerson cut in sharply, "or I'll call the police."

Paul's mouth was still open. He clamped it shut and glared at her. The tiny woman glared back, and what composure Paul had faded quickly. He turned and left without a word.

When he had gone, Miss Emerson looked at Lauren.

"Are you all right, dearie?"

"Yes, thanks to you."

"It's good to be independent," Miss Emerson said, "but now and then everyone needs a little help." And, having made that pronouncement, she disappeared into her apartment.

Within minutes, Kobelski rapped softly on Lauren's door.

"Boy, am I glad to see you," she said as she let him in.

"I'm glad you're glad. What did Bernstein want?"

"Paul? You know him?"

"I know *of* him. What was the problem?"

Lauren explained. "He's usually moody, but tonight he was worse than I've ever seen him. His mood just kept changing."

"Something set him off," Kobelski said mildly. "Any idea what it was?"

She told him that Dr. Herbert had reprimanded Paul that afternoon. "I wouldn't want to have him jump on *me* like that," she said.

"But this wasn't the first time?"

"No, that's true."

"Anything else happen today?"

"No——" She suddenly remembered how Paul had been watching her that afternoon. "It really bothered him that I'd changed my hair. He seems to think I'm playing up to Dr. Herbert. And tonight he talked about women using men. Kobelski, you don't think Paul's the killer, do you?"

He shrugged his broad shoulders. "We'd better watch him carefully."

"I guess you're right," she said. "I haven't had any supper yet. Would you like to have an omelet with me?"

"Sounds good." He made himself comfortable on the sofa. As she worked in the little kitchenette, she saw him pull his packet of photographs from his wallet. One in particular seemed to fascinate him.

As she made a fresh pot of coffee and prepared a green salad, she realized that this was the first time in a month that she'd shared a meal with anyone. How isolated she'd become! Her whole life had narrowed to just work and school and at both she had only casual acquaintances.

"Supper's ready!"

Kobelski looked up.

"Ellen?" she asked as he returned the photograph he'd been studying to his wallet.

He nodded.

"Did you know her?"

He stood up and loosened his tie. "No, not really," he said slowly. "But I wish I had."

Lauren recognized the ring of truth in his reply. But if he hadn't known Ellen, why did he seem almost obsessed by her picture?

"Do you always spend so much time brooding about the victims in your cases?"

An odd look flashed across his face for an instant. "Not always. This one's different."

"Why?"

"Because," he snapped. "Because she was too young and too pretty and had too much to live for!" He looked at Lauren and frowned. "And because I've known her father for a long time."

"I'm sorry."

"That's all right." He glanced at the little table. "Let's eat. It looks good." He took off his sport coat and shoulder holster and hung them on the back of the chair before sitting down.

"Are you going to buy some clothes tomorrow?" he asked.

"Mm-mm. I have to meet with my professor in the morning. I thought I'd go shopping in the afternoon."

"Fine." He sprinkled his omelet liberally with pepper.

"Kobelski, have the police checked out the guys Diane and Ellen dated? Was there anyone who knew both girls?"

"They've checked as much as they could. And no, so far they haven't been able to come up with any guy who knew both girls personally."

"Of course," Lauren thought out loud, "with Diane working in the Nite Owl, anyone could have struck up an acquaintance with her. And if she went out with him afterward, who's to know? I mean, she lived alone."

"Right." Kobelski sighed. "The modern young woman. The possibilities are wide open."

"Did Ellen live alone, too?"

"She shared an apartment with another girl, but the girl was out of town for a whole week before the murder."

"So if Ellen had become friendly with a fellow in that last week, no one is likely to know that, either."

"Right again. And the university is so big that most students have their own little circle of friends and everyone else is a stranger."

"But the girls must have had some close friends!"

"Apparently not the kind they confided in."

"That's hard to believe!"

"Is it? If *you* had a personal problem right now, who would you go to?"

There was no one, of course. "Am I so much like them?"

Kobelski sipped his coffee. "Let's just say you're the perfect bait."

When they had finished, he rose and started clearing the table. "You cooked," he said. "I'll clean up. Fair enough?"

Lauren smiled. "Who am I to pass up a good deal!" Resting her feet up on the vacant chair, she watched him as he rolled up his sleeves and filled the dishpan.

"Tomorrow night," he said over his shoulder, "I want you to spend the evening in the Nite Owl. Just hang around and see what happens."

"Alone?" Lauren made a face. "I'm not used to going to bars alone."

Kobelski turned around with a soapy salad bowl in his hand and grinned. "Well, it's time you got liberated."

"Oh, swell! And suppose somebody tries to pick me up?"

"Great! Let him." But when he saw the look of dismay on her face, he added, "Don't worry. I'll protect your life *and* your honor."

Suddenly she looked very troubled. "This man, the murderer—he doesn't rape his victims, does he?"

Kobelski shook his head. "There's no evidence that he does."

When he had finished drying the last of the dishes, he hung up the dish towel carefully and turned to Lauren. "You have any scissors?"

"Of course. Why?"

"Bring them here."

Her sewing basket was in the bedroom. When she returned with the scissors, she saw that he had rifled her kitchen drawers. On the counter lay three steak knives, a paring knife, a bread knife, a skewer, an ice pick, and a meat fork.

"What are you doing?"

"Getting rid of potential weapons. This guy is supposed to try to strangle you, and I don't want him to change the script."

"I really don't see what difference it makes if I'm stabbed or strangled to death."

He stopped what he was doing and looked at her. "There's a *damned* important difference, Ellen! It takes three or four minutes to strangle someone. But one stab wound in the right place and that's it!"

The scar on his face became more noticeable when he was upset. It seemed to grow whiter. Actually, Lauren thought, it was probably because his face was flushed and provided a greater contrast to the scar tissue.

She sighed. "Yes, you're right. I might be able to defend myself against a strangler—" She paused. "There's a fire ax in the hall. Should we get rid of that, too?"

"Uh-uh. It can't be removed from the box without setting off the alarm. I checked. I think we only have to worry about things that he might pick up on impulse."

Kobelski found an empty grocery bag and dumped all of

the sharp objects he'd collected into it. Then he looked around to make sure he'd gotten everything.

Lauren picked at a fingernail. "I don't think I did a very good job of handling Paul tonight," she said finally.

"You did fine."

"But I was afraid to let him into the apartment. I never really gave him a chance to try to kill me. Maybe we missed our chance to catch him!"

He smiled. "Ever been fishing?"

"No." She wondered what that had to do with it.

"Takes patience." He strapped on his shoulder holster and buttoned his sport coat. "If Bernstein's our man, he'll be back." He picked up the bag and left.

Later, Lauren lay in the darkness of her bedroom and tried to sleep. Something was wrong. She punched up her pillow and turned over, looking for a comfortable position. She tried to keep her mind free of unpleasant thoughts, pushing away every mental image that came to her. But from somewhere in the back of her mind, she heard Kobelski's voice saying, "There's a *damned* important difference, Ellen!"

Ellen. He'd called her Ellen.

If it had been just a slip of the tongue, why did it frighten her?

She slept with the light on.

CHAPTER EIGHT

There was one thing nice about having such a small apartment, Lauren thought. It didn't take long to clean. The day was sunny and so unusually warm that she opened all the windows to air the rooms.

As she changed her bedding, Lauren noticed a small tear in one of her sheets. It would have to be mended before she used it again.

There were times when she couldn't help comparing her present life with the one she might have had if she'd married Doug. He had a good position in his father's prosperous electronics firm. When they learned that Doug had asked her to marry him, his parents had announced that their wedding gift would be the down payment on a new house. And Doug had given her a lovely ring—a family heirloom—a pear-shaped diamond surrounded by tiny opals.

Lauren shook her head at the memory. *Where did you ever find the guts to turn it all down?*

That was more than fourteen months ago. In fact, she thought with a pang, at the end of the month it would be a year since she learned that Doug had become engaged to Nancy McAllister. She remembered reading the announcement in the paper. She'd studied the picture of Nancy and thought what an attractive couple they made. Doug's dark good looks contrasted with Nancy's fragile features and honey-colored hair.

Lauren looked around her little apartment and consoled herself. Her life had its rough edges, but at least it was her own. The decisions were *hers,* and that was important. And it was a lot better than being relegated to the role of decorative wife. That was what Doug had wanted. A pretty, gracious hostess to impress his clients.

She recalled one of their last quarrels.

"But Doug, if we live in Waterville, I won't be able to go to graduate school."

He'd looked at her with the manner of an adult giving candy to a child. "But you won't *have* to go to school anymore! Surely you realize there's plenty of money. Lauren, you're going to be a lady of leisure."

Lauren had tried to keep the irritation she felt out of her voice.

"Don't you understand? I *want* to work!"

"Oh, you'll be plenty busy. There'll be the Women's League and the Jaycettes. Since I'm in business, that's only good public relations. And, of course, the country club. Don't worry, you won't be bored, darling."

She hadn't answered him. She remembered fingering her ring, trying to tell herself that it would work out even though she knew deep down that it was all over between them.

After Lauren finished cleaning the apartment, she took a quick shower. Then she fussed with her hair. Some strands just wouldn't stay in place. She finally got it right and began to apply her makeup.

It was like being an actress, she thought. Get all the costumes and props together and then go out there and play your part.

If only I could be sure how the last act comes out!

The door of Professor Bell's office was open. Lauren saw him standing by the window talking on the phone, his back to her. He, too, was wearing a costume—tight Levi's, a baggy gray sweater, and moccasins.

He turned as he put down the phone and saw Lauren. "Ah, Miss Walker—Lauren. May I call you Lauren?"

Without waiting for a reply he reached into his desk and took a roll of breath mints from a drawer. He popped one into his mouth and offered one to her. When she refused, he took her gently by the shoulders and led her to one of the chairs in front of his desk.

"Do sit down while I get your records," he said amiably. He turned to one of the filing cabinets.

Lauren sat on the edge of the chair and waited in silence while he rummaged through the drawer.

"Ah, yes." Bell finally turned around with a manila folder and leafed through several of the papers in it. "You've been doing quite well until now. Exceptionally well, in fact. I was very impressed with your work. That's why I was disturbed by the results of your last quiz." He handed her the paper.

She began to read. Bell had not commented upon the content but had simply written in the margins where he had taken off points for each answer. Lauren's heart sank as she read her final grade. Sixty-five. "I'm afraid I don't understand what you wanted," she said slowly.

He pulled another chair close to hers and sat down so that their knees were touching. "Well, let's take a closer look." He leaned toward her as he examined the first page of her work.

Lauren couldn't be sure whether he was being deliberately obnoxious or whether he was one of those people whose personal space was so small that he felt comfortable only when he was physically near another person.

"Now," he was saying, "this is what you reported seeing on that first slide. The bronchial epithelium. Here, I have an enlarged photograph you can look at for comparison." He went to his desk and searched through the papers piled on the top of it until he found what he wanted.

Lauren had correctly identified the type of cells pictured in the photo as well as all the components of the cell. Yet Professor Bell had taken off ten points. She looked at him. "I don't understand what I did that was wrong."

"It wasn't what you did, it was what you didn't do," he said quietly. "Look at this area of the photograph. What do you see?"

"That's the cytoplasm." She'd labeled it as such.

"Yes, of course," he said a trifle impatiently. "But does it always look like that?"

Lauren considered. "It does look a bit strange."

"Exactly! And that's what I wanted you to say. As a matter of fact, this is a sample of diseased bronchial epithelium. I didn't expect you to diagnose the disease, but you should realize that it is not normal epithelium."

He looked at her. "If you were working somewhere, say a hospital or a research lab, and that sample came to you for analysis, your failure to spot that abnormality could cost a human being his life."

Lauren flushed. He was right, of course. How could she have been so stupid? And yet the instructions had said only, "Tell me what you see." She hadn't realized that Professor Bell was asking for more than simple identification.

"And this one," he went on, turning to another of her answers. "You correctly labeled all of the chromosome pairs but failed to see that one of the chromosomes was broken. A person exhibiting this karyotype has a good chance of producing abnormal children. It's important to realize exactly what you are seeing—or not seeing."

Lauren nodded. "I understand, Professor Bell. I guess I didn't think deeply enough about what I was doing."

He smiled warmly. "Deeply enough—exactly! You have a good mind, Lauren. You can be a top-notch scientist, but you need someone to guide you through the rough spots. I would be willing—in fact, *more* than willing—to work with you personally."

His face was so close to hers that Lauren could feel his breath. Was this the veiled proposition that Nedra was talking about? Or was he simply being nice? A concerned teacher who wanted to help a student?

"What do you suggest?" she asked.

"We might get together now and then—for a couple of hours in the evening—and, um, just talk things through. You'd be surprised how helpful that can be."

Lauren wriggled with discomfort. "Thank you very

much, Professor Bell, but I don't think I could manage the time right now. I work several evenings a week. Perhaps if I study harder——''

"Ah, yes." His pale blue eyes grew cold. "Perhaps that would be sufficient." He paused a moment. "Just remember, Lauren, you need to put more of yourself into your studies." He got up and replaced the manila folder in his file.

As Lauren rose to leave, he turned to her and the cold look in his eyes was gone. He took her arm and said, "You may reconsider. Please know that I am always available. I realize that you did your undergraduate work at a small college and may not have all the background you need to compete with students here. I'd really like to help."

Lauren felt her cheeks growing hot. Nedra had been right. Bell certainly chose his words carefully. It wasn't what he said, it was how he said it. He could always claim she'd interpreted his words in the wrong way.

She struggled to keep her voice as natural as possible. "Thank you. I appreciate your wanting to help me. And I certainly will come to you if I have any more trouble."

"Very good, Lauren. I shall see you in class on Monday. And by the way, I haven't complimented you on your change of appearance. It's most flattering."

She ate lunch in a nearby drugstore and debated Bell's motives.

Suppose he *had* been making a pass. That didn't necessarily mean anything would happen to her if she ignored it. There were lots of girls on campus who'd jump at the chance to date a professor, especially one as good-looking as Bell. Maybe that was his way of sounding her out without asking outright. It would save him face if she refused. Just because Bell dated coeds didn't necessarily mean he blackmailed them into going out with him.

By the time she finished eating, Lauren had decided that Nedra's warning had been unnecessary. She felt considerably better and was determined to put the whole matter out of her mind for the time being. She'd been looking forward to shopping and that was what she was going to do right now.

She headed straight for Nina's, a smart little shop she'd been in once. By the end of the afternoon she'd picked out two pairs of slacks, two blouses, a sweater, a skirt, and a pair of shoes. There was nothing left of Kobelski's five hundred dollars.

It was nearly six when she returned to her apartment building. Miss Emerson spotted her in the foyer and insisted on returning several of Lauren's plants.

"Don't they look much better? I rather think they're relieved to have a little breathing room. Of course, you won't really be able to tell the difference for a week or two. Then watch them grow!"

She clucked contentedly and insisted on selecting the proper place in Lauren's apartment for each plant. "No, no! Now, that's why your fern wasn't doing well, dearie." She clicked her tongue over a sickly plant in a bright red pot. "Ferns are very susceptible to drafts. It would do much better over here."

She placed the pot carefully on top of the dust cover of Lauren's record player. Lauren would have to move the plant every time she put a record on. But she knew better than to protest. It would be less trouble to rearrange the furniture than to argue with Miss Emerson.

"I'm going to keep your spider plant for the time being. It's quite sick and Lloyd's kitchen window is just the spot for it. You haven't been giving it enough sun." The last sentence was spoken in a tone that would have made a saint cringe with guilt.

"Oh, I know," Lauren apologized. "I kept meaning to get a hanging planter so I could put it in my bedroom window. There's more sun there."

Miss Emerson shook her head. "Northeast? It's not the best exposure for a spider plant. Still, I suppose it's better than the living room. That tree doesn't let much light in here, does it?"

Lauren bit her lip. Sometimes Miss Emerson was too much!

"I see you've been shopping," the little woman said, evaluating Lauren's packages. "Did you find anything nice?"

Happy for a chance to divert her from the plants, Lauren smiled. "Yes. Would you like to see?"

She put on a cream-colored blouse and a pair of tailored brown slacks.

"Very nice," Miss Emerson said approvingly. "I do wish we'd been allowed to wear slacks when I was your age. But you need something—a touch of color, perhaps. Do you have any scarves?"

Feeling like a little girl with an overprotective mother, Lauren got out her box of scarves.

"Oh, here's one that would look good," Miss Emerson crowed, holding up a brown, gold and orange print. "And this is the way you should wear it." She carefully arranged the scarf at Lauren's throat.

As she looked at herself in the mirror, Lauren realized that Miss Emerson had been right. The scarf was just the thing she'd needed. In addition to the note of color, it softened the neckline of her blouse. The outfit would be perfect to wear tonight to the Nite Owl.

Later, as Lauren was leaving the apartment, she paused in front of the mirror for a last-minute check. Then she realized why the scarf seemed so perfect.

In one of Kobelski's photos, Ellen Rickover had been wearing a similar outfit. In fact, Lauren had consciously selected these clothes because they were so much like Ellen's. But what she hadn't remembered was that Ellen had been wearing a brightly colored scarf at her throat.

Of course, Miss Emerson couldn't have known that. It had to be a coincidence.

CHAPTER NINE

Lauren hesitated outside the Nite Owl. What if she couldn't find a vacant table? She didn't want to end up on a barstool. This wasn't going to be easy!

"Not watching where you're going again?"

As she turned, she saw the friendly face of the sandy-haired fellow she'd collided with yesterday. Tonight he was wearing a sweatshirt with an outsize telephone number printed on it.

"If you're looking for some company, the selection of guys in there isn't so hot. You'd be much better off grabbing me." He crooked an elbow at her and winked. "The name's Terry Wells, ma'am."

For a split second Lauren wondered whether Kobelski would approve. Then she thought, *Why not? He sent me here to get picked up, didn't he?*

"I'm Lauren Walker." She gave him her most dazzling smile as they went in.

Before her eyes had a chance to adjust to the darkened interior, she heard several voices calling out above the jukebox music and the buzz of the crowd.

"Hey, Terry!"

"Here we are!"

"C'mon over!"

Terry grinned at her. "Sounds like our table is waiting."

A moment later, he said, "Lauren Walker, meet Angie, Bets, Foxy Freddy, Kelso, and Pudge.

Five genial faces greeted her from a round table set with two foaming pitchers of beer, several glasses, and a huge bowl of popcorn.

The husky, bearded individual named Pudge rolled his

eyes and groaned. "Terry, how come you always end up with the gorgeous girls?" He stood up and bowed to Lauren. "Pleased to make your acquaintance, my little ravioli." In a conspiratorial whisper, he added, "If you get bored with that handsome jerk, I'm available." He gave a sigh of mock anguish. "I'm *always* available!"

Terry laughed. "Don't mind Pudge. The sight of a pretty girl does strange things to him."

Lauren chose a seat which gave her a view of most of the crowd. And, she thought, it gave the crowd a view of her. Kobelski would probably call it dangling the bait.

Terry signaled to a barmaid. "Another pitcher and two more glasses, please." He turned back to Lauren. "These three fellows share an apartment with me. They may appear to be moderately insane, but don't let that fool you—they're completely crazy."

"Thanks for warning me." Lauren smiled. "I hope you'll satisfy my curiosity," she said to the baby-faced redheaded fellow across the table. "Why do they call you Foxy Freddy?"

"My name is Freddy Fox——"

"But he's a little backward," Pudge finished.

Good-natured laughter rippled around the table.

Lauren looked around. The Nite Owl was a fairly large room, but low ceilings and amber lights gave it a cozy atmosphere. There were owls everywhere: sketches and photos of owls on the walls; ceramic owls in front of the mirror behind the bar; stuffed owls, some toy and some real.

"You look familiar." The tall, angular girl named Angie was evidently nearsighted. She squinted at Lauren across the small table. "Have I met you before?"

"I don't think so, but you may have seen me on campus. I have classes at the science building three mornings a week."

Angie looked doubtful.

Foxy Freddy leaned forward. "I know why she looks familiar." He turned to the others. "She looks like Dee Dee."

"Who?" Lauren asked.

"Dee Dee! Of course!" the tiny gamin-faced girl named Bets exclaimed. Her bangs kept falling into her eyes and she pushed them to the side as she turned to Lauren. "Diane Towle. She used to work here. Maybe you heard about it. She was murdered."

"Hey!" Terry cut in. "That's not a nice thing to say to someone you've just met. Let's have some happy talk."

"No, wait," Lauren said. "If you don't mind, I'd like to talk about it." It seemed a good idea to learn all she could about Diane. "You see, someone else told me that I resemble another girl who was murdered recently."

Freddy frowned. "Yeah! The Rickover girl. I remember now. Her picture was in the paper. You look even more like her."

"Oh, that's weird!" Bets cried.

Kelso, the dark, bookish young man who hadn't spoken until now, grunted. "I don't know about this other girl, but you really do look like Dee Dee. I can say that because I knew her personally. Went out with her a couple of times."

Angie looked at him. "You never told me that!"

"That was last spring, before I even met you." He turned to the rest of them. "The police gave me quite a time after she was killed. I was darned lucky my dad had taken me on a fishing trip the weekend of the murder."

"You mean you had an alibi?" Lauren asked innocently.

Kelso grinned. "Iron-clad! My father and two of his business associates and the guide were with me the whole time." He shook his head and whistled through his teeth. "I've always hated fishing and went only to please my dad. But it would have been a real hassle if I hadn't gone!"

"I remember now," Foxy Freddy said. "They didn't find her body right away, so they couldn't pinpoint the exact time of the murder."

"Right!" Kelso replied. "If I'd stayed on campus, there's no way I could have accounted for every minute of that weekend."

"How much did your father pay for the alibi?" Pudge teased.

Kelso bristled. "Don't be ridiculous!"

"It's not ridiculous. Everyone knows your father is loaded. And we all know he'll give you anything you ask for. Actually, I'm surprised that the police haven't thought of that."

Kelso's face darkened. He stood up and rolled his shirtsleeves to his elbows.

Pudge looked at him in alarm. "Hey! Joke, buddy! It was only a joke!"

Kelso glowered. "Then your sense of humor is pretty *sick!*"

There was an uncomfortable silence around the table for a moment, and Lauren turned to Terry. "What was Dee Dee like?"

He looked at her appraisingly. "I don't think she looked that much like you. I mean, she had the same color of hair and maybe she was about the same height, but——" He shook his head. "I can't put my finger on it. You're different, that's all."

"I'll tell you what Dee Dee was like," said Pudge, meditatively stroking his beard. "Va-va-va-voom! That's what she was like!"

"Oh, come on!" This was Bets. "She wasn't all that sexy!"

Foxy Freddy regarded her with amusement. "Spoken like a jealous woman."

"I am not jealous! I liked Dee Dee. She was cute and friendly. But that's all."

"You didn't see her at the talent show!" Pudge looked over at Terry. "*You* saw her, didn't you?"

Terry grinned. "Sure did! She was something else that night!"

Pudge leaned across the table and addressed Lauren. "Picture, if you will, a beautiful blonde like yourself, poured into a slinky red gown with a pul-*lunging* neckline. The lights are low. The spotlight is on Dee Dee, and she's singing in her breathy little-girl voice, '*I wanna make love to you, baby. Right now.*' Now that's sexy!" He closed his eyes and smiled at the memory.

"Hmph!" Angie sniffed. "It's not hard to see why she got killed!"

Kelso put his hand on hers. "Aw, Angie, come on! It was just part of her act! Dee Dee was a nice girl."

"Nice girls don't get strangled!" Angie retorted.

"They do when the strangler's a psychotic," Foxy Freddy put in. "And that's what this guy had to be."

Terry refilled Lauren's glass. "Freddy's our house psychologist. He's majoring in psych. An analysis, please, Dr. Fred."

Freddy borrowed Kelso's glasses and let them slide to the tip of his nose. "Dr. Sigmund Fred, iff you plees." He leaned back in his seat and pursed his lips for a moment. "It iss my considered opinion," he said slowly, "dot dis murderer hates vomen! Particularly beautiful blonde vomen like *you*, mein dear." He leaned forward and placed his hand upon Lauren's.

She stiffened.

"Cut it out, Freddy!" Terry put his arm protectively around Lauren's shoulder. "That's not funny!"

Freddy flushed, his freckles temporarily seeming to disappear. "Hey, I'm sorry. I didn't mean to scare you. Really! I guess I just didn't think."

He was so genuinely apologetic that Lauren couldn't help feeling sorry for him. "It's all right, Freddy. It really doesn't bother me. Actually, I've gotten kind of interested in the murders."

"Good!" said Kelso. "Because I want to ask Freddy something. Serious question: If this guy just hates women in general, was it a coincidence that the two victims looked so much alike?"

Freddy shrugged. "I wouldn't try to second-guess a psychotic. It could be a coincidence."

Angie frowned. "And if it's not?"

"Then he's probably killing someone else in his mind."

"Maybe it's a ritualistic thing," Kelso offered. "A subconscious cry for help. Isn't that how somebody explained the Boston Strangler's killings?"

Bets pushed her hair out of her eyes again. "It could be that he doesn't even remember killing them. Like Dr. Jekyll and Mr. Hyde."

Pudge hooted.

"It does happen," Bets said defensively. "That guy in Chicago—the one who killed eight girls—I heard that he didn't remember a thing!"

"Maybe he's another Jack the Ripper," Terry suggested. "All of the women that he killed were prostitutes. So maybe there's something that the victims do that makes him kill."

"Like what?" Angie squinted at him.

"How should I know?" Terry looked around helplessly. "I was just tossing out a suggestion."

"It could be anything," Freddy said seriously. "Remember that case in Michigan? That guy killed several girls, *and every single one of them had pierced ears!*"

Pudge looked at him sideways. "Maybe I've had too much beer, but what does *that* prove?"

"Only what I said in the first place. He's *crazy!* And I *still* think he's killing somebody else in his mind."

Kelso took back his glasses. He put them on and frowned. "Damn it, Freddy! You got the lenses all greasy!"

Freddy looked guiltily at his hands. "Buttered popcorn," he muttered. "Sorry."

Kelso dipped a corner of his napkin into his beer and rubbed the lenses with it. He held the glasses up to the light and frowned.

Pudge put his arm out and caught a passing barmaid around the waist. "*Hel*-lo, you ravishing bundle of pulchritude!" He pulled the girl onto his lap. "I have a deep and burning need within me that only you can satisfy, darlin'."

The girl looked at him knowingly. "More beer, right?"

Pudge gave her a good-natured grin and pushed an empty pitcher toward her. She departed and returned shortly with a full one.

Lauren looked around. The Nite Owl's crowd was mostly young and noisy, and in a particularly good mood tonight because the football team had won an upset victory that afternoon. Every so often, one little group or another would burst into the school fight song, which ended with half the singers cheering while the other half chug-a-lugged their beer.

Just a bunch of happy young faces, she thought. Was one of them the mask of a murderer? She looked around for a likely suspect and realized that a young man at the bar was watching her in the mirror. He was of average height, she guessed, though it was difficult to judge when he was sitting down. His medium-brown hair was slightly too long to look neat and his expressionless face was long and narrow. He wore a navy windbreaker with the collar turned up. His gaze met Lauren's in the mirror for a moment, then he looked quickly down at his beer.

"Hey! No fair leaving me, even if only in thought!" Terry was smiling at her. "What's on your mind?"

She smiled back. "I was wondering, is this—" she ran her finger across his chest—"your telephone number?"

Terry grinned. "Of course! It's a gimmick. All four of us have one of these. And every day, one of us has to wear his shirt. There's a calendar in the kitchen with a regular schedule on it."

When Lauren looked incredulous, Pudge said, "He's telling the truth! But he didn't tell you about the graph we've plotted to keep track of how many phone calls we get from new girls each day. It's a real status symbol to have the graph zoom up the day after you've worn the shirt." His face suddenly filled with gloom. "Of course, Terry has the record."

Lauren laughed. "You mean the girls *actually* call?"

"You bet!" Pudge smirked. "Women's liberation is the greatest thing to come along in years."

"And do you go out with all of these girls?"

Kelso answered. "That's how I met Angie! Actually, we've got a system. When the girl calls, we ask her what day she saw the shirt. Then we know which fellow she's interested in. He gets first choice. If he talks to her on the phone and thinks he'd like to go out with her, okay. If not,

he tells her he's busy but one of his buddies is available."
He shrugged. "It all works out."

"I don't *believe* it!"

Terry smiled at her. "It probably sounds juvenile, but it's all good fun."

"Oh-oh!" Bets said *sotto voce*. "Look who's here!"

Without turning her head, Lauren looked toward the door. Professor Bell had just entered, his arm around a young girl. Lauren recognized her from cytology lecture. She knew the girl had not been doing well in class.

"Earning her grade for this semester," Angie sniffed.

"He's in here nearly every weekend." Foxy Freddy said. "And with a different girl each time."

Bets shuddered. "I can't think of anything more horrible than going out with him. I hear he's weird!"

"Some people say *I'm* weird." Pudge smiled at Lauren. "I'm not, really. I'm just a big lovable teddy bear."

"Well, *big*, at least!" Terry teased.

"You know, it wouldn't surprise me if Professor Bell were the guy who killed those girls," Angie said slowly. "I mean, he's in here all the time. He would have known Dee Dee. And the other girl was a student, wasn't she? He could have met her on campus."

"That's a possibility," Freddy said seriously. "He was married, you know. His wife left him. Maybe he's subconsciously killing her."

"You mean he doesn't know he's the killer?" Bets asked.

"Well, I wouldn't go as far as that," Freddy said. "He could have alternate personalities——"

"If he has two personalities, they're *both* rotten, believe me!" Angie muttered, fingering her bracelets.

"Did you ever have him for a class?" Lauren asked.

"Yeah! Biology, my freshman year. I dropped the course halfway through the semester. He intimated I was going to flunk unless I had some 'special tutoring,' if you know what I mean!"

Lauren's heart sank.

"Well," Pudge sighed, "that's one way to get dates."

"Oh, knock it off," Terry said. "To listen to you, anybody'd think you'd never gone out with a girl. I happen to know that you've been out with at least six different girls this month."

"And I had to ask every one of them," Pudge said morosely. "What I want is for women to fall at my feet adoringly."

Kelso groaned and turned to Freddy. "Analyze that fellow, Doctor."

"Let Terry do it. My office hours are over for the evening."

"An analysis?" Terry asked. He furrowed his brow, stroked an imaginary goatee and gazed intently at Pudge. Finally he nodded.

"Dis iss der verst case of insecurity I haff ever seen! Vot he needs iss a varm blanket und a puppy dog."

Everybody laughed except Pudge. "I did have a dog once," he said with exaggerated solemnity. "But he ran away."

"Aha!" Terry exclaimed. "Dot proves my theory!"

"It doesn't prove anything!" Bets objected.

"Yes, it does," Pudge said. "It proves we all need another beer." He picked up the pitcher and began pouring refills.

Kelso held out his glass.

"Are you sure you want any more?" Angie asked, putting her hand over his glass. "You'll end up with a headache tomorrow."

"My headaches aren't from drinking," Kelso said irritably. "I told you that the doctor said what I eat or drink has nothing to do with it."

"But——"

"Angie, don't start telling me what to do. Who do you think you are, my mother?"

She flushed. "Sorry."

Lauren chose that moment to glance around again. The fellow at the bar was still looking at her in the mirror. This time he did not look away. He sipped his beer and returned her gaze, his face still expressionless. It made Lauren uncomfortable and she turned in her chair to face the door.

He was, she decided, a little older than most of the students in the Nite Owl. Twenty-five or twenty-six, perhaps.

Professor Bell and the girl he was with got up to leave. The girl was a little unsteady on her feet and had a haunted look on her face. Bell looked smug.

"I feel sorry for her," Bets said.

Angie sniffed. "You needn't. She doesn't have to do it. Dropping a course or even flunking it isn't the worst thing in the world."

A moment later, Lauren noticed that the fellow who'd been watching her was gone.

CHAPTER TEN

"May I take you home?" Terry asked as the group began breaking up shortly after midnight.

"Thanks," Lauren said, "but my car's just a block away."

He considered a moment. "I walked here. I could drive you home in your car and take a bus back to the apartment."

Lauren smiled. "If you're willing to go through all that, I won't say no."

Outside, they discovered that the skies had cleared and the temperature had dropped sharply.

"Brr! It's six blocks from my place to the bus stop," Lauren warned. "It'll be a chilly walk! Are you sure you want to go through with this?"

"Oh, yes, ma'am!" He took her arm as they crossed the street.

"But aren't you cold?"

He smiled. "Only on the outside," he said softly.

When they reached her car, Lauren offered him the keys and he unlocked the door for her.

"I like your friends," she said as Terry started the engine.

"Yeah, they're a good group—easy guys to live with."

"I can see that. This evening was fun."

"So it was. Now, where do you live?"

Lauren gave him directions.

"I know a long cut. Got any objections?"

She laughed. "Can't think of one."

The campus bordered a lake and Terry headed the car down the shoreline drive. Ahead of them and to the left, the city lights reflected in the water.

"Actually," Terry said, "there was one thing wrong with the evening."

"What's that?"

"Everybody else did so much talking, I didn't get to find out anything about you."

"There isn't much to tell. I'm a part-time student and a full-time technician at Kincaid. And you?"

"Oh, I'm a full-time student. I'm working on a Ph.D. in economics."

"Sounds interesting."

"Actually, it's awfully boring, lots of dull statistics. And don't change the subject. Tell me about yourself. What's your family like?"

"I'm an only child," Lauren said slowly. "I—I lost my father when I was three."

Why had she put it that way? Even now, couldn't she admit that he'd left her?

"Hey, me, too! I'm an only child and I kind of lost my father when I was little. My folks were divorced, you see." He looked at her. "I know how it is."

Take any problem, Lauren thought, and you're never the only person in the world with it.

"You're being quiet again," he said. "What's on your mind?"

"I was thinking about that girl—Dee Dee."

"Oh! Say, I'm sorry they kept bringing the subject up. It must have made you uncomfortable."

"It didn't really bother me," Lauren stretched the truth. "I just wondered what she was like. Did you know her?"

"Not personally. But I saw her every time I went into the Nite Owl, and the other guys and I go there a lot. She seemed like a nice girl. You know, friendly. Always smiling. I knew Kelso had gone out with her a couple of times."

"Only a couple of times? I was under the impression that he knew her pretty well."

Terry laughed. "Kelso never goes out with the same girl for long. He's terrified of getting involved. He's been seeing Angie for almost two months now, and that's got to be his record.''

Lauren steered the conversation back to Diane Towle. ''Would you say that she was—well, your type?''

He looked at her. ''That's a strange question!'' He considered for a moment. ''No, I wouldn't. She struck me as the type of girl who'd be happiest when she was all dressed up and in a room full of celebrities. Me, I'm at my best in an old pair of jeans. A roaring fireplace and rain on the roof.'' He smiled. ''How about you?''

''Positively the rain on the roof for me.''

''Beautiful!''

Lauren studied his profile as he swung the car back toward town. He had a strong chin, and a mouth which looked as though he were going to laugh at any moment. His eyes were wide and clear with a hint of amusement in them. His lightheartedness was contagious, she realized. He was fun to be with. For that matter, everyone had been fun.

There hadn't been many carefree evenings in her life. Not many hours spent laughing and joking with other people her own age. Even Doug had been a serious, intense person. She felt suddenly old. How much she'd missed!

Be careful, she warned herself. *Start wallowing in self-pity and you'll end up just like your mother.*

She looked at Terry, who winked back at her. He reached over and squeezed her hand.

When they arrived at her building, he parked her car and they hurried into the foyer to escape the night chill.

''I really enjoyed the evening,'' Lauren said. ''Would you like to come in for a bit?''

For a moment their eyes met. There was a question in his. Then he glanced at his watch. ''If I run, I can make the crosstown bus, and there's not another one for a couple of hours. Can I take a rain check?''

''Sure.''

''Good! And by the way''—his eyes were twinkling—''I always kiss on the second collision.''

There had not been many men in Lauren's life. Nor many kisses. But she knew instinctively that there was something special about Terry's kiss. It was incredibly gentle. He made her feel like some rare, delicate flower which must be handled only with great care.

She looked up into his face. His eyes were so wide and clear, she thought. Like a little boy's.

"Lauren," he said softly.

"Yes?"

"Just Lauren. It's a pretty name."

She'd never given much thought to it. Ma had simply chosen the name of her favorite movie star, Lauren Bacall. It was okay, but nothing special. Until now. When Terry said it that way, it was beautiful.

Then the spell was broken. "Gotta dash!" he said, giving her hand one last squeeze.

From her living room window, she watched Terry sprinting in and out of the shadows as he headed for East Hamilton Avenue and the bus stop. She felt warm and happy. The evening had turned out very nicely, she thought. Not at all what she'd expected. Of course, Kobelski might not be pleased. Somehow she felt he hadn't intended for her to spend the evening drinking beer with a friendly group of college kids. Still, he couldn't complain. She'd sat there in plain sight. If the murderer had been in the Nite Owl, he couldn't have helped seeing her.

She slept until after nine on Sunday morning. As she made her breakfast, she found she could not keep Terry Wells out of her thoughts. She'd never before been so immediately attracted to a man. But then, she'd never met anyone like Terry before. Lauren wondered what he thought of her. Obviously he had plenty of dates. To him, she might be just another girl. But the way he'd kissed her—did he kiss all the girls that way?

She cleared the breakfast dishes off the table and took out her books. There was an exam coming up in cytology on Wednesday.

But it wasn't easy to put Terry out of her mind. She very much wanted him to like her. Funny about his being an only child too, she thought. And not having a full-time father, either. That hadn't seemed to bother Terry as much as it had her. Maybe his mother wasn't like Ma. That could make a lot of difference. His mother was probably a lively, cheerful person.

It wasn't fair, she thought with a trace of bitterness.

She pored over her notes. Remak and Virchov. Sutton's chromosomal theory of inheritance. Schleiden and Schwann. Page after page of enormously magnified pictures of cells, each with organelles carefully labeled. She studied each one diligently. No mistakes this time. She'd recognize any abnormality!

There was a knock at the door. "It's Jane Emerson, dearie!"

"I just wanted to tell you," she said after Lauren had opened the door, "there was a young man here last night looking for you."

Lauren looked at her, puzzled. "Did he leave his name?"

The little woman shook her head. "No. He just asked if this was where you lived. I said it was, but you were out for the evening. So he said he'd come back another time."

"What did he look like?"

"Tall, very nice-looking!" Miss Emerson beamed.

It wasn't much of a description, Lauren thought with exasperation. But it really wasn't important. If he was coming back, she'd find out who he was and what he wanted. She thanked Miss Emerson and went back to her books.

She had read over all the test material and was reviewing it when the phone rang.

"Lauren?" Her pulse quickened as she recognized Terry's voice. "I wondered whether you'd like to have supper with me tonight? I know a nice little Italian restaurant. . . ."

After that, she found it impossible to concentrate. She shook her head and sighed. She was acting like a teenager. But it was time for a break anyway—almost two o'clock.

She'd take a walk. She needed to get some fresh air.

The Petries were packing their car for a picnic. The little girls' wide dark eyes sparkled with excitement. Their ponytails bobbed up and down.

"It's so late already! It's not worth going!" Mr. Petrie grumbled as he loaded the picnic basket in the trunk of the car.

"Oh, honey, please!" Mrs. Petrie handed him a blanket. "You don't have to go to work tonight, and the girls will enjoy it so much—even if it's only for a couple of hours."

Lauren smiled at the little domestic scene, but inwardly she wanted to cry out, "Take your daughters and enjoy them, Mr. Petrie! Give them this afternoon. You may not remember it twenty years from now, but they will."

The happy chatter of the children faded away as Lauren walked down the street. It was a crisp fall day, but the sun was warm and accented the brilliance of the foliage. On the vacant lot on the corner, a group of boys were playing football. It wasn't until she was several blocks from home that she realized there was no one in sight. Where was Kobelski? He said he'd be watching her all the time except when she was in class or at work. But what about weekends? He couldn't spend all weekend without any sleep! He couldn't possibly guard her every minute!

Was that a footstep? She looked around but couldn't see anyone. Her heart started to race. *Don't be a dope*, she told herself. *This guy doesn't kill girls on the street in broad daylight.* All the same, she quickened her pace and turned toward East Hamilton, where there was always traffic.

It was hard to get used to being watched all the time. She'd become very conscious of people looking at her. Like the fellow at the bar last night. He was probably just a lonely person who was people-watching for lack of anything better to do and had settled on her. How many times had she singled someone out in a crowd and watched him for no particular reason?

And then there was Kobelski. Somewhere. Invisible. He

probably knew what she'd had for breakfast. Had he seen Terry kiss her last night?

Last night, she'd felt other eyes, too. Terry's friends looking at her and seeing the resemblance to Dee Dee. Someone—was it Freddy?—had remarked that she looked even more like Ellen than Dee Dee. Probably every time she went on campus, someone's head turned because she resembled the two dead girls.

Had their murderer spotted her yet? Would she know him when she saw him?

East Hamilton Avenue was alive. Sunday afternoon traffic was light, but children on bicycles and skateboards zipped in and out among pedestrians. Young mothers pushed their babies in strollers and buggies. Pigeons searched the gutter for tidbits. The world was normal again.

She was passing a branch of the public library when an idea occurred to her. Libraries kept files of back newspapers, didn't they? With curiosity suddenly welling within her, she started up the steps.

Inside, the building was cool and quiet. Not many people spent their Sunday afternoons in the library.

"We keep only the recent copies of newspapers here," the librarian told her.

"How recent?" Lauren asked.

"Six weeks. If you want to go back further than that, you'll have to go to the main library, where the microfilm files are kept."

Six weeks. Dee Dee Towle had been killed more than six weeks ago, but not Ellen Rickover. "I'd like to see the back copies that you have here, please."

The librarian showed her the rack where the old newspapers were kept. Lauren settled herself at a table and spread them out in front of her. Ellen's murder was on the front page. There was a picture of her—one which Lauren recognized. It was among Kobelski's photos. She glanced through the article.

Ellen's body had been discovered on a Sunday evening

by her roommate, Brenda Selms. Brenda had last seen Ellen ten days earlier when she—Brenda—had left for California to attend her sister's wedding. According to the medical examiner, Ellen had probably been killed sometime on Saturday afternoon. Cause of death: strangulation.

Ellen was described as a bright girl beginning her second year of college as an art major. Her teachers were quoted as saying, "She had enormous potential," and "She was serious about her studies," and "She appeared to be a nice girl—the type who never gets into trouble." Ellen's father was described as a prominent Chicago businessman. There was no mention of her mother. The police were questioning the dead girl's friends. They had no suspects at present.

A tag line at the end of the article mentioned that another coed had been strangled several weeks before, but no mention was made of the physical resemblance between the two girls. Nor was it suggested that both crimes might have been committed by the same person.

Follow-up articles on Ellen's murder revealed nothing new. The police were still questioning suspects, and had no definite leads. Lauren was disappointed. She had hoped that the newspapers would tell her something she did not know.

She was putting the newspapers away when she realized that she now knew the name of Ellen's roommate.

Brenda Selms was listed in the telephone directory, but when Lauren dialed the listed number, she got a recording. "The number you have dialed is no longer in service."

Of course. Brenda had probably moved. She certainly wouldn't want to live in the place where her roommate had been murdered. But maybe Brenda hadn't left town.

Lauren dialed Information, but the operator told her that they had no new listing for Brenda Selms.

Now what? Was Brenda a student? The newspaper hadn't mentioned it, and, as far as Lauren could remember, neither had Kobelski. But it was worth a try.

Lauren called the main number of the university. Brenda L. Selms, the disinterested voice of the operator told her, was listed in the student directory. She gave Lauren the number, and Lauren realized with a feeling of elation that it was not the one listed in the city directory. She promptly dialed it and a young woman answered.

"May I speak to Brenda Selms?"

There was an instant wariness in the voice at the other end of the line. "Who is calling, please?"

Lauren hesitated. "Lauren Walker. I—I'm an old friend of Ellen Rickover's," she said self-consciously. She had never been good at lying.

"Oh! Oh, sure. Hey, Bren! It's for you."

Ellen's former roommate had a soft musical voice. "Ellen never mentioned you," she said slowly.

"Perhaps not," Lauren said quickly. "We—we hadn't seen each other since high school graduation. But I would like to talk with you. Please? It's important."

There was a pause. "Okay. When?"

"This afternoon?" Lauren suggested hopefully.

"Why not? Do you know where I live now?"

She gave Lauren her address and directions.

Lauren ran most of the way back to her apartment building to get her car.

CHAPTER ELEVEN

Brenda Selms's new apartment was in a large security-locked building at the edge of campus. She'd said apartment 312, and when Lauren pressed the buzzer button, she recognized the soft musical voice that came over the speaker.

"Who is it?"

"It's Lauren Walker. I called a little while ago."

"C'mon up."

A click released the inside door and allowed Lauren to pass into the inner building.

The door to 312 was opened by a thin red-haired girl of twenty or so. She wore wire-rimmed glasses and Levi's with a gingham overblouse. Her hair was parted in the center and fell in rather frizzy waves to her elbows. When she saw Lauren, she gasped. Her pale complexion grew even whiter beneath her freckles.

"El——" She covered her mouth with her hand. "Oh! For a moment I thought——"

"I'm sorry," Lauren said. "I didn't mean to frighten you."

"You look just like her!"

"I know." She hesitated. "May I come in?"

Brenda blocked the door. "You weren't a friend of Ellen's, were you?" she asked suspiciously.

Lauren shook her head. "I owe you an apology there. It's just—people have been telling me that I look like her. I'm beginning to feel haunted."

The red-haired girl softened her expression. "I can see why. Come in."

"Did you have any trouble finding the place? I—I moved after—it happened. I couldn't live there anymore. Janie—a friend of mine—let me move in with her. She's the one who answered the phone.''

The apartment was small and furnished with serviceable contemporary furniture. It was obvious that the occupants were students, for there were several shelves filled with textbooks. A typewriter sat on the kitchen table along with a ream of paper and more books. A periodic table of the elements was taped to the door of the refrigerator.

''How did you get my number, by the way?'' Obviously, Brenda still had some misgivings about this talk. ''The phone's in Janie's name.''

Lauren explained.

''Of course, I forgot that the university would have my number.'' She relaxed a little. ''Why don't you sit down? Want a Coke?''

''Yes, thanks.'' Lauren sat on one of the straight-backed chairs beside the table. ''Brenda, I came here hoping you'd tell me about Ellen. What she was like. Who she knew. The kinds of things she did or didn't do.''

Brenda filled a plastic tumbler and set it in front of Lauren. ''Why do you want to know?''

Lauren's mind raced. ''Because—because it's really getting on my nerves having people tell me how much I resemble her. I guess I need reassurance that I'm me, and not her.'' She paused. ''There's curiosity, too. I keep wondering what she was like.''

Lauren had chosen her words well. Brenda relaxed. ''I can understand that.'' She filled a glass for herself and sat down opposite Lauren. ''There's not much to tell. Ellen was a nice girl. Really smart, too. She started college at sixteen, you know. She was allowed to skip freshman English and she went right into an advanced lit course. That's where I met her. We became pretty good friends. When the girl I was sharing an apartment with decided to move out, I asked Ellen if she'd be interested in taking her place. She jumped at the chance. She'd been living in a dorm and she wanted a place where she'd have room to paint. She was an art major.''

"I know," Lauren said. "Do you have any of her work here?"

"I have one of her drawings. The police took her sketch pad, and her father sent a moving company to take away the rest of her things. But come and see what I managed to save." She led Lauren into a bedroom.

Hanging on the wall above the bed was a large charcoal drawing of a nude woman in a garden. Standing, half-turned, beneath a tree, she was reaching for one of its branches.

"Ellen did it in her life drawing class. It's called *Eve*, of course. She did an *Adam*, too. We had both of them hanging side by side in our living room. But the *Adam* was destroyed at the time of the murder." She turned to Lauren with an expression of defiance on her face. "By rights, I suppose *Eve* belongs to Ellen's father, but I kept it. I wanted something to remember her by, and I don't think he'd appreciate it. He doesn't deserve it anyhow."

Lauren was puzzled. "Why do you say that? Didn't she like him?"

"Oh, Ellen never talked about him much," Brenda said as they returned to the kitchen. "But you could see—I mean, he never wrote to her, even though she wrote to him every week. He'd send her a big check regularly, usually with a note written by his secretary. I saw a couple of them. 'Your father says he's glad you're enjoying your basic drawing class. He misses you.' I mean, how do you think Ellen felt? Her mother was killed in a car accident when she was twelve, and there were no other children." There was bitterness in Brenda's voice. "He was all she had. And yet he couldn't take a minute to write two sentences himself."

"Did you ever meet him?"

"Uh-uh. Once, he was supposed to come down from Chicago. It was Ellen's birthday and he—I mean, his secretary had said that he was coming here to take Ellen out to dinner. Ellen seemed very excited about it. But at the last minute, a messenger showed up at the door with a dozen long-stemmed roses and a note that said he'd been called away on business and he was sorry. Happy birthday!"

"How did Ellen react?"

Brenda laughed harshly. "Better than I did! I was furious to see her being treated that way. But she just shrugged it off. I suppose she was used to it."

"Did she have many friends?"

Brenda shook her head. "Ellen didn't seem to want anyone to get close to her. I knew her as well as anyone, and I never really understood her. Although she got along well with people, she preferred to be alone most of the time. She was always studying or sketching something."

"Did she date at all?"

"In a casual way. Mostly to the movies or campus doings—a couple of times we went to apartment parties or had kids over here for a pizza and beer. She didn't seem particularly interested in any one guy. I'm sure she wasn't sleeping with anyone."

"You were gone the week before the murder, weren't you? She could have met someone during that time."

Brenda nodded. "My sister's wedding—I was her maid of honor. The summer session was over and fall registration hadn't begun yet, so I spent the whole week—actually ten days—with my family in California. But I don't think Ellen got involved with anyone during that time. She had built walls—really thick walls—around herself. It would take more time than that to get close to her."

"Who do you think killed her? And how did he get in?"

"Why, she let him in, of course! It had to be some fellow she wanted to sketch."

"I don't understand."

"It was funny," Brenda said, shaking her head. "In some ways, Ellen was so sophisticated, and yet she was such a child, naive and trusting. If she saw somebody on the street who had an interesting profile, she'd just walk up to him and ask if she could sketch him." Brenda smiled. "Of course, most people were flattered by that. A lot of them sat for her."

"Do you mean she invited them to your apartment?"

"Sometimes. It depended. If it was a nice day and they both had time, she might do her sketching outdoors on campus. At other times, she'd just set up an appointment and they'd come to the apartment."

"Only boys?"

"Oh, no! Girls, too. And little children with their mothers." Brenda laughed. "Once I came home to find an old man—in overalls and a fisherman's cap—sitting in the living room. He did make a lovely picture." She looked at Lauren. "You see, when Ellen saw someone, she saw a model—something to be sketched or painted. She never considered them, well, *personally*."

"I'm not sure I understand."

The condensation from Brenda's glass of Coke had made a little puddle on the table, and she dipped her finger into it and traced a design on the table top.

"Well, for instance, once she invited a married professor over to sit for her. I didn't think that was a good idea and told her so. She didn't seem to understand. 'There's nothing wrong with doing a sketch of him,' she said." Brenda looked helplessly at Lauren. "I'm not a prude, but she was such a child sometimes. I didn't want her to get into something she couldn't handle. But when I tried to explain to her that people might talk, that the professor's wife might not like it, and so forth, Ellen just laughed. 'You worry too much!' she said. 'Ninety-nine percent of all the people in the world are very nice. They're not going to make up stories about me that aren't true.' "

"The professor—what was his name?"

"Nelson. From the art department. I had to tell the police about him."

"You say the police took her sketchbook?"

"Yes, but it won't do them any good."

"Why do you say that?"

"Because the last two drawings were torn out." She looked straight at Lauren. "The person she was sketching was her murderer. I'm sure of it. He tore out those drawings of himself so no one would know he'd been there.''

Lauren sighed. "But you say she had all kinds of people sitting for her! Then it could have been a student or a faculty member or someone who had no connection with the university.''

Brenda shrugged. "It could have been anybody.''

"The other sketch—*Adam*—you said it was destroyed at the time of the murder. Why?''

"Who knows? The person who killed her tore it off the wall and tore it—it was only mounted on pasteboard—into little bits. Then he threw the pieces all over—all over Ellen's body." Brenda suddenly went pale.

"Why? It was logical to remove the drawing of himself from the sketchbook, but why tear up the other drawing? What happened to the pieces?''

"The police took them.''

Of course. They would. Maybe Kobelski knew more about it. She'd ask him.

Brenda was staring at her. "Well?''

"Well, what?''

"Does any of this answer your question?''

Lauren had to think a moment before she realized what Brenda was talking about. "Oh, about us being alike. I'm afraid we were more alike than I realized.'' And they were. Ellen had lost one parent and was alienated from the other. She'd had no close friends. Her studies had apparently been her whole world.

"I'm afraid for you,'' Brenda said suddenly.

"Why do you say that?'' Lauren felt her heart quicken.

The other girl shook her head. "I'm not sure. I have the feeling—when I saw you in the hallway, I almost thought you were a ghost. Even now, I don't feel you're quite real. Something's wrong.'' Brenda played with her empty glass for a moment. Then she said in a low voice, "My grandmother on my mother's side was Irish—that's where I got my red hair—and she always claimed she knew when something terrible was going to happen." She paused and looked directly at Lauren. "I don't mean to frighten you, but right now I think I know how she felt. Please be careful." It was a plea. She was entirely serious.

Apprehension was contagious, Lauren realized, and she tried to shake it off by quickly changing the subject.

"Mr. Rickover—do you know anything more about him?"

"Only that he's rich and that he's the meanest man alive!"

Lauren raised her eyebrows. "Something Ellen told you?"

"No. Like I said, she almost never talked about him. I think—I think it hurt too much. And Ellen was the type who kept her hurts to herself."

Like me again, Lauren thought. "Then why do you say he was mean?"

"He *ignored* her! I lived with Ellen for three-and-a-half months, and he called her once on the phone. The entire conversation didn't last more than two minutes. He was sending some papers for her to sign. As I understood it, from this end of the conversation, she inherited some money when her mother died and her father managed it for her."

Brenda looked indignant. "That was all. No 'How are you?' or 'Are you feeling all right? What's happening?' Just 'I'm going to send you these papers and I want to be sure you understand what to do with them.' "

"But a lot of parents are like that," Lauren said. "They get all wrapped up in their work or"—she thought of Ma—"or their worries. Particularly when their children get older and don't need them every minute."

"But how many parents don't have time to come to their child's funeral?" Brenda demanded.

"*What!*"

"I'm not kidding! I don't know whether he even came here after she—was killed. *I* never met him anyhow. After the autopsy, the police released her body to a local mortuary. The people there were supposed to make arrangements for sending Ellen—her body—back to Chicago. When I called them to find out if there would be any kind of service here, I was told that the funeral hadn't been scheduled yet! That they had orders to 'keep her on ice' until Mr. Rickover notified them!'' Brenda's fingers tightened around her empty glass until her knuckles grew white. Tears of anger formed in her eyes. ''That bastard! It's been over three weeks since she died, and she's still lying there!''

CHAPTER TWELVE

Lauren's mind was not on her driving as she headed back to her apartment. She was stunned. How could any man do that to his daughter?

It was five-thirty when she parked her car in front of the building. Terry had said he'd pick her up at seven. It was a good thing she had a little time to mentally unwind. She was too keyed up and confused to be good company. Maybe some aspirin—for a moment, she wished for tranquilizers. Then she thought of Ma and changed her mind. *Better to endure it and learn to handle my problems.*

She was making herself a cup of tea when she heard a soft, familiar knock on the door.

"Busy little thing, aren't you?" Kobelski said with a touch of sarcasm as he entered. He carried a thick book in one hand. "How come you went to see the Selms girl?"

"I was curious. What's wrong with that?"

He glared at her. "Didn't it occur to you that if our man is watching you, he might think something's fishy when you visit Ellen's roommate?"

"You mean he'd guess I'm baiting him?"

"Maybe."

"I never thought of that."

"You should have."

"I'm sorry. Do you think I blew the whole thing?"

His expression softened a little. "Probably not. But don't do anything so stupid again!" He tossed the book on the table.

Lauren winced. She didn't like being called stupid. But Kobelski was right. Now that she thought about it, it had been foolish to go to Brenda's apartment.

"And another thing," he went on irritably. "You spent half the day here. Why? I want you *visible.*"

"I've still got to study, Kobelski."

"You can study on campus."

She drew a deep breath and let it out. "Okay, I will. I apologize again. Are you through picking on me?" Lauren suddenly realized that her lower lip was protruding in defiance. *I must look like a stubborn little kid,* she thought. She began to smile. At the same time she noticed amusement sneaking into Kobelski's eyes, and at once they both broke into laughter.

"Bygones?" he asked.

"Bygones. Want some tea?"

He wrinkled his nose. "You got any coffee?"

"If you'll settle for instant."

"Sure. Who was the fellow you were with last night?"

"Terry?" She was conscious that her feelings had crept into her voice when she'd said his name, and she quickly turned to the sink to fill the kettle with water.

"Joe College," Kobelski said.

"His name is Terry Wells. He lives in an apartment near campus with three other fellows. One's named Freddy Fox, another is called Kelso—that's probably his last name—and the third I only know as Pudge. They all hang around the Nite Owl a lot. Kelso even dated Diane Towle."

Kobelski's eyebrows went up. He consulted his notebook. "Kelso, Richard. Right. He was cleared in the Towle case. Fishing trip."

She put the kettle on and turned to him. "Is there any chance that Kelso's alibi isn't rock-solid?"

"Why do you ask?"

"Last night, one of the other fellows—Pudge, I think—hinted that Kelso's father had paid his fishing partners off to provide his son with an alibi. Pudge said it as a joke, but Kelso took it hard. Protested too much, I thought."

"Good girl." Kobelski scribbled something in his notebook. "Okay, what else do you have for me?"

"A Professor Nelson from the art department. Married. Brenda says Ellen invited him to sit for her at their apartment. Brenda said she told the police about him."

He grinned. "She did. They questioned Nelson. His wife was less than thrilled to hear that he was in a coed's apartment when he said he had been doing research on a pre-Renaissance painter."

"Does he have an alibi for the day Ellen was killed?"

"Water-tight—for the whole weekend. He was attending a conference in Denver. He has plenty of corroborating witnesses, hotel receipts, airline records, everything."

"So he's in the clear?"

"Uh-huh. Anything else?"

"Angie—she dates Kelso—said something interesting. When she saw Professor Bell—he teaches the course I'm taking—come in, she remarked that he'd be a good suspect. He dates students a lot and he's often in the Nite Owl. He would have known Dee Dee—Diane. Maybe he knew Ellen, too."

"Yes, he did know Ellen. Bell teaches freshman biology during the spring semester. Ellen was in his class last year. What else do you know about him?"

"That he's brilliant. He wrote my cytology text, and I know it's good. It's used in half the colleges around the country."

Kobelski nodded. "Yeah. And his freshman course is popular. He had two hundred and fifty students last spring."

"There are courses like that on every campus," Lauren said. "Undergraduates are usually required to take so many credits of a general science. Word gets around when a teacher is good and his class is interesting."

"Which means Bell gets to meet a large proportion of the undergraduate coeds every spring."

"Not necessarily," Lauren declared. "I've taken courses like that. When there are a couple hundred students in a lecture, you might never get to meet the professor. If you've got questions or need help, you end up with a teaching assistant. And they're usually the ones who administer and grade the exams. Ellen could have taken Bell's course and never come closer to him than the last row of seats in the lecture hall.''

Kobelski shrugged. "Maybe."

The teakettle whistled, and Lauren poured hot water into two cups, adding instant coffee to one and dropping a teabag into the other. "You take it black, don't you?"

He nodded and sat down at the little table. "This Bell—what was he doing at the Nite Owl?"

Lauren set his cup in front of him. "He was with a girl—a girl from my class, as a matter of fact."

"How old is he, would you say?"

"Fortyish, I think. He seems older than you."

Kobelski grinned. "Thanks. There are days when I feel older than everybody. I've had a lot of them lately."

"You ought to take less violent cases."

He sobered. "I'll remember that."

"I'm sorry," Lauren said quickly. "I forgot Mr. Rickover was your friend."

"I didn't say he was a friend," he said evenly. "I said I've known him for a long time."

"Oh." She considered a moment. "Kobelski, what's he like?"

His eyes narrowed. "Why?"

"Brenda says that—well, she doesn't like him."

"Has she ever met him?"

"No. But she says that he wasn't close to Ellen at all."

He sipped his coffee. "A lot of parents aren't as close to their kids as they'd like to be."

"According to Brenda, he just didn't care about Ellen."

Kobelski flushed. "That's not true," he said quietly. "He cared. Only maybe he forgot to show it."

Lauren didn't say anything.

"Tom's wife died a few years ago," he went on, "and he—went to pieces. He—kind of buried himself in work to forget."

"That's the only burying he's done lately," Lauren said sharply.

"What are you talking about?"

"You *must know!* Ellen's body is still in the morgue. What kind of a creep would leave her like that?"

Kobelski flushed again. His scar stood out white against his cheek. "Tom's no saint," he said angrily, "and there are some things about him that I don't like, but he's not Satan, either!" He gulped the rest of his still-steaming coffee. Then he got up and rinsed out his cup in the sink. "Look, we just work for him. I'll do my job. You do yours."

Lauren felt put down. "I'm sorry." She was apologizing a lot lately. "I guess it isn't any of my business."

"You're right," he snapped. "It isn't!"

He walked over to the sofa and sat down. In a few moments he was himself again.

"We were talking about Bell," he said. "You say he dates students quite often?"

"I gather that he does." She got up and moved over to the living area. "Funny thing, I think he's interested in me."

"How so?"

Lauren explained. "But I'm not completely sure. One minute I think he's sincere and that he honestly wants to help me. He *is* a marvelous teacher. But then he'll say something—and it's the *way* he says it that makes me wonder——"

Kobelski leaned forward. "Then here's what you're going to do: You go tell him you've changed your mind. You'd like to talk about the problems you're having with your work. Let him take it from there. If he wants to go out with you, agree."

"Do I have to?"

He gave her a fierce glance.

"All right, all right. I'll do it. And by the way, I'll need more money."

"Blew the whole wad, huh?" He looked amused.

"It wasn't hard."

He pulled out his billfold. "I've only got a couple of hundred on me." He handed her four fifties.

"Oh, there's no hurry," she said, feeling a little guilty. "I won't have time to go shopping again for a few days, anyhow."

"Keep it anyway. You can never tell when you'll need it."

Lauren folded the bills carefully, then unfolded them. "There's something else I wanted to ask you about."

"What's that?"

"Brenda said that the—the killer tore up one of Ellen's sketches and scattered the pieces over her."

"That's right."

"I wondered about the model. Who posed for that sketch? Brenda said it was done in class."

"He was a professional model. The police have already checked him out. He's in the clear."

"But *why* would the murderer do that? Tear up the picture, I mean?"

He shook his head. "I don't know, but it seems it's part of his crazy pattern."

Lauren looked at him.

"I have information that says he also tore up a sheet of music and threw the pieces all over Diane Towle's body."

"It sounds like you're not sure about it."

"I'm reasonably sure. My source is pretty good."

She frowned. "But why should there be *any* doubt? The police could tell you whether it's true. You're working with them, aren't you?"

He smiled and said with exaggerated patience, "A private detective works with the police only to a point."

"I don't understand. You're both on the same side, aren't you?"

"Sure. But just my presence is an embarrassment to them. It reminds them that somebody doesn't think they're doing a good enough job."

"But you said—I mean, I thought—aren't they helping you at all?"

He shrugged. "I keep in touch with them. Because I work for Ellen's father, any information they'd give him, they give me. Beyond that, I have to find out things for myself."

"But something like the sheet of music—why shouldn't they tell you about that?"

"Plenty of reasons. First of all, they want to be the ones to crack the case. It gives them an advantage to have clues that I don't have."

"Why, that's stupid! No wonder it's so hard to catch criminals!"

Kobelski smiled. "That's the real world, doll. But don't think too badly of Captain Hunnicut. There are other reasons for withholding information."

"Such as?"

"Such as being able to tell whether or not someone is telling the truth when he confesses to the killing."

"But if he confesses——"

"Not everybody who confesses to a crime is guilty. Do you know how many people have already admitted to killing one or both girls?"

She stared at him.

"It happens all the time. Some people just need to be punished and they're willing to be punished for anything, even crimes they didn't commit."

"So if somebody confesses and can't tell the police about the sheet of music, they know he's not the right guy." Lauren felt suddenly tired. "The whole world is full of crazy people."

"But very few are evil-crazy. They're mostly sad little people with their own private hells." He looked depressed. It was strange the way his face responded to his moods. He could be fierce or gentle, frightening or—Lauren smiled to herself—very attractive.

"You're a lot of different people, Kobelski."

"I live in a lot of different worlds, doll."

"I wish you didn't have to live in the world of evil-crazies."

He looked pained. "And I wish I didn't have to drag you into it."

"Hey!" she said lightly. "Nobody dragged me. I'm in it for the money, remember?"

He appeared not to have heard her. "Sometimes you act a lot older than you are."

Lauren made a face. "Thanks a lot!"

"I mean it as a compliment. A lot of twenty-two-year-olds are still kids."

She looked away. "I had to grow up fast." It was true. Even in elementary school, she often felt that she was the grown-up and her mother the child. There had never been a carefree time in her whole life. That was the difference between her and Terry and his friends.

"Feeling sorry for yourself?"

She smiled. "Runs in the family."

"But don't you see? You're one of the lucky ones."

"*Lucky!* Why?"

"Because you *did* grow up. A lot of people have unhappy childhoods, and then spend the rest of their lives tied up in knots. They become the crazies." He reached over and picked up the thick book from the little end table. "I've been trying to construct a psychological profile of our man, and this book has been very helpful. I think it would be a good idea for you to look through it."

"A little bedtime reading, is that it?"

"Something like that. Anyhow, the first thing I learned was that men who commit multiple murders of females almost always have an arrested emotional development."

Lauren tried to follow his line of thought. "And that comes from an unhappy childhood?"

He nodded. "And there's generally a poor relationship with a female figure somewhere."

"Too bad we can't just go around and ask every man we suspect whether he had a happy childhood."

Kobelski slowly shook his head. "Chances are you wouldn't learn a thing."

"Why not?"

"Because really troubled people often don't know that they are."

"They have a distorted perception?"

"Right. They might honestly believe they've had a reasonably happy life."

"So how do we get at the truth?"

"I'm depending on you to pick that up." He put the book back on the table. "By the way, did you learn anything else from Brenda?"

"Probably nothing you don't already know. That Ellen often asked strangers to sit for her and sometimes brought them to the apartment. And that one of them is probably the killer because the last two pages were ripped out of her sketchbook. Have you seen the sketchbook?"

"Yeah. Captain Hunnicut let me look through it. The police are checking out everybody they can identify from her sketches."

"But the killer tore out *his* picture."

"Still, you can't leave any loose ends. Everyone who posed for her has to be checked out."

"Anybody we know among them?"

"Bernstein's in there."

"*Paul?*" Lauren blinked. "Why didn't you tell me? Isn't that important?"

"Probably not. The drawing of Paul was done outdoors. In front of the fountain by the library. There's no reason to believe he was ever in her apartment."

"That doesn't mean he wasn't."

"No, but there were forty-two other men sketched in that book. Bernstein's really only one fellow in a crowd."

"I suppose you're right. Besides, if Paul had come to Ellen's apartment to sit for her a second time, he would have torn out the earlier picture as well as the recent ones, wouldn't he?"

Kobelski grinned. "He could have forgotten about it. *or*

he might have thought that we'd think what you're thinking and left it in on purpose.''

Lauren laughed. ''Don't confuse me. Besides, I know Paul. I don't think he's capable of such subtle thinking.''

''There's another possibility,'' he said softly.

''What's that?''

''He might not have recognized his own picture. A lot of people don't.''

''Distorted perceptions, you mean?''

He nodded.

She sighed. ''I wish this weren't so complicated.''

''Murder nearly always is.''

''I suppose so.'' She looked at her watch. ''Oh, my gosh! It's nearly seven. I've got to get ready.''

''For what?''

''A dinner date.''

''Joe College?'' Kobelski seemed mildly amused. ''Have we got something going here?''

''His name is Terry,'' she said with some irritation. ''You told me not to discourage any man who showed an interest in me. And this one's interested.''

''Apparently.'' He grinned at her as he got up to leave. ''Stay visible.'' He glanced at the book. ''And don't forget to do your homework.''

CHAPTER THIRTEEN

When he had gone, Lauren picked up the book and glanced at the title. *The Psychology of the Mass Murderer*.

Thumbing through it, she found that it was almost a medical text, full of complicated explanations, diagrams, and technical terminology.

"Wonderful bedtime reading," she thought sarcastically.

Terry arrived promptly at seven, wearing a sport coat and tie and driving a shiny red MG.

"Wow!" Lauren exclaimed when she saw it. "That's a beauty!"

"It's Kelso's. His dad gave it to him for his birthday," he said. "My car's making strange noises. I think something under the hood is about to die. Anyhow, Kelso said we should be his guests."

He held the door open for her and she slid into the leather-upholstered bucket seat.

"Some birthday present!" she said. "I guess Pudge wasn't kidding when he said that Kelso's dad had money."

Terry shrugged. "Kelso's family is—well, funny. His dad's in construction and has his good years and his bad years. When times are good, he spends money like it hurts to hold it. On the other hand, Kelso told me there were times when they ate nothing but beans for a week at a stretch because there was no money. His folks broke up because of that."

Terry turned on the stereo tape deck as soon as he started the engine. "This car comes with the best of everything." He grinned at her.

"I'm surprised Kelso isn't using it," she said. "What's he doing, studying?"

Terry shook his head. "Uh-uh. He's in bed with a terrible headache."

"Too much beer last night?"

"No. He was feeling fine this morning. He's been getting these headaches for a few months now. They're really bad. He can't stand light, and any amount of noise seems deafening to him. He gets this glassy look in his eyes and locks himself in his room with the lights out and a pillow over his head."

"How awful! How long do the headaches last?"

"Usually only for a couple of hours. Sometimes longer."

"That almost sounds like migraine."

"That's what the doctor thought at first, but then he changed his mind. Kelso's supposed to go in for some more tests in a couple of weeks."

The restaurant was a few miles away from the campus and it catered to a well-to-do clientele. In the center of the dining room was a marble fountain with water cascading down over colored lights. Potted trees and hanging plant-filled baskets made it seem as if they were dining in a garden. Soft mandolin music wafted through the room. The tables were covered with red and white checked cloths.

"Like it?" Terry asked.

"It's lovely, but it looks expensive."

He laughed. "We can live it up tonight. I won the poker game last Wednesday evening."

"It doesn't sound as though much studying goes on in that apartment," Lauren observed.

"I'll take the fifth on that," Terry said good-naturedly as the hostess led them to a tiny table in a corner.

They ordered linguini with clam sauce—Terry said it was the best thing on the menu—and while he studied the wine list Lauren found herself thinking about Kelso.

His childhood had not been completely happy. He seemed to have remained on good terms with his father after his parents split up. Did that mean that he didn't get along with his mother? Did he have the kind of personality that

Kobelski was looking for? Or was she just jumping to conclusions?

"You're far too solemn this evening," Terry said.

"I'm sorry. I was thinking about a conversation I had this afternoon with a friend."

"And was it so serious? Maybe you ought to talk about it. It won't do your digestion any good to eat with a frown on your face."

Lauren smiled. "It wasn't anything important, really. We were talking about childhood experiences and how they affect one's personality."

"I see." He rearranged the salt and pepper shakers. "And that bothers you because your childhood wasn't particularly happy."

"Why do you say that?"

He flushed. "Sorry. I assumed that your father's death was pretty hard on you."

Why had she lied to him about that? She really ought to tell him the truth. It wasn't her fault that her father had walked out on them. She didn't need to be ashamed.

"It was hard on you, wasn't it?" Terry looked at her with concern.

She nodded. Because she felt guilty about not correcting her story, she added, "But it wasn't that bad. I mean, a lot of kids only have one parent. You, for example."

"That was different," he said. "After all, my dad didn't die. And my mom was great. She really stuck by me. We lived with my grandparents for a few years while Mom was trying to make ends meet."

The waiter brought the wine and waited for Terry's approval before filling their glasses. When he had gone, Lauren said, "It must have been hard for your mother."

"Oh, Mom's pretty resilient. She always took care of herself. And me, too," he added. "How did your mom manage?"

Lauren hesitated. She couldn't tell him about Ma's depressions and drinking problems. "As well as could be expected, I guess,'' she said evasively. ''She loved him a lot.''

''What was he like? Do you remember?''

The question took her by surprise. Impressions flooded her memory. ''He was tall. Very tall.'' Had he been? Or did it only seem that way because she had been so little? ''And he had dark wavy hair that fell across his forehead when he laughed.'' Where had that memory come from? Or was her mind playing tricks on her? ''He used to give me piggyback rides every night before I went to bed.'' *That* she remembered clearly.

''What did he do for a living?''

She took a deep breath. Had her mother ever told her? Funny—how could she not know what kind of work her father had done? Hadn't someone once said, ''When your father was on the road?'' She exhaled very slowly. ''He was a salesman.'' Why had she said that? Why couldn't she admit that she didn't know? ''I'm not sure what he sold.''

But if her father had been ''on the road''—away from home—at times, he couldn't have given her piggyback rides every night, could he? Had it really happened only once or twice? When her father had been there, she had been happy, hadn't she?

''Did your mom remarry?'' Terry was asking her.

''No, she never did.''

''That made it hard on you, didn't it?'' Terry was looking at her closely. ''I mean, she probably leaned on you a lot.''

''Not really.'' Lauren winced. How could she lie like this? She remembered the times when she'd had to cook their meals because her mother was in no condition to do so. Once—she'd been only nine—she spilled a steaming pot of soup and burned her leg badly. She had screamed and screamed, but Ma was sound asleep. Little Lauren had limped into the bedroom and tugged at the inert figure lying there on the bed. But there was no response. Lauren had finally called her Aunt Lil, who lived across town.

When Aunt Lil arrived, her face dark with foreboding, she took one look at the empty pill bottle beside Ma's bed and called an ambulance. They took Ma away in a swirl of flashing lights and screaming sirens. Terror supplanted the pain of Lauren's burn. She sat wordlessly as the doctor in the emergency room dressed the wound, smiled at her and spoke some encouraging words.

After that, Aunt Lil had come to live with them. She kept track of Ma's pills, doling them out only as needed. She took over the cooking and cleaning. The house looked better, but it wasn't any happier. The shades were always drawn, as if to hide some terrible secret.

"Hey! You keep wandering off and leaving me." Terry was smiling at her.

"Oh! I'm sorry." Lauren started guiltily. "What were we talking about?"

"You said your mother hadn't ever remarried."

"That's right. No, she didn't. Did yours?"

A fleeting expression crossed Terry's face. For a moment, Lauren wondered whether she had touched upon too painful a subject. But Terry's good-natured grin was back in a flash.

"Yeah, she did. When I was fourteen."

"Were you unhappy about that?"

He shrugged. "I don't suppose any boy wants another man to take his father's place. But Joe's okay. He takes care of Mom and pays the bills and he never gave me a hard time."

"But it wasn't the same as having a father?"

"I wouldn't really know. Even before the divorce, my old man wasn't around much." He looked abstractedly across the room. "I guess what really bothered me was that my grandparents—Mom's folks—didn't approve of Joe. There was a big argument and they never spoke to my Mom again. I go and see them sometimes, but they won't even mention her."

"That doesn't seem fair!"

"It isn't. Families ought to stick together, don't you think?"

"Oh, yes," Lauren said with an intensity that surprised

even herself. "I mean, no matter what differences people have, they should be able to work things out."

Terry smiled at her. "We think alike, don't we?"

In the soft light of the restaurant, Lauren couldn't be sure whether Terry's eyes were blue or green. But whichever color they were, they were undeniably attractive. She felt herself drawn to Terry in a way that she had never experienced before—except for Doug.

She looked up at Terry quickly. Did they think alike? "Twenty questions," she teased. "Do you think a woman should have a career if she wants to?"

He seemed surprised. "Why not?"

"It might mean that a man would have to cook once in a while—I mean if he had a wife who worked."

He laughed. "Big deal! Who do you think does half the cooking in our apartment now?"

"You?"

"Pudge and I cook, Foxy and Kelso clean. It works very nicely." He looked at her mischievously. "Of course, we *do* eat out a lot. And the apartment isn't exactly spic and span all the time. But we manage. I'm not a stickler for such details, anyhow."

"Then it doesn't bother you if a woman is ambitious?"

"No. Why should it? Of course, I wouldn't want to see her completely neglecting her family, but I think there's room in a woman's life for a family and a career if everyone cooperates."

The waitress arrived with the dessert menu.

"You have to try the almond shortbread," Terry insisted. "It's fantastic."

And it was. As she sipped a steaming cup of espresso, Lauren asked, "Did you get a lot of phone calls today?"

His eyebrows went up.

"Because you wore the shirt yesterday," she explained.

"Oh, that!" He laughed. "The phone rang off the wall. But do you know something?"

"What's that?"

"The right girl didn't call. I had to phone her myself."

Lauren flushed.

"Don't you believe me?"

"You must date a lot of girls," Lauren said, avoiding his gaze.

"I *have* dated a lot," he admitted. "And I've had my crushes and infatuations. But I've never been in love. Have you?"

Lauren hesitated. Had she? If she had really loved Doug, wouldn't she have chosen him instead of her own plans and ambitions? "I thought so once, but I'm not sure now," she said slowly.

"Then perhaps we both have something to look forward to," he said softly. He pressed his finger to his lips, then reached over and lightly touched hers. His finger barely brushed her lips, but Lauren found the gesture strangely moving. She looked across the little table at him and felt that she was looking at the other half of her own soul.

As they left the restaurant, Terry said, "I know you have a long day ahead of you tomorrow and I've got a problem set to finish before tomorrow morning, so I think we'll call it an evening, okay?"

Lauren smiled. "Sure."

He shook his head. "You're supposed to say, 'Sure, on one condition.' "

She looked at him uncertainly. "What's that?"

"On the condition that we do this again, soon."

She laughed. "I'm all for that."

It was shortly after ten when they reached her apartment building. They found Miss Emerson on her knees in the foyer, wiping the linoleum with a damp rag. She looked up at them.

"Don't mind me!" She laughed. "I was carrying out the garbage and my bag split open. What a mess!"

Lauren looked at Terry.

"Don't mind me!" Miss Emerson said again cheerfully and went on wiping the floor.

Lauren grimaced and said under her breath, "She's an old busybody. She'll never leave while we're here. Shall we go in?" She looked toward her apartment door.

Terry grinned at her. "You know the best way to handle busybodies, don't you?" he whispered. "You give them something to remember! Follow my lead."

Aloud, he said dramatically, "My darling! I can't live without you!" He threw his arms around her in a theatrical embrace and kissed her, leaning her backward until she was nearly off-balance. His kiss ended with a smack that resounded through the foyer.

Miss Emerson stared.

"Come with me to my hideaway on the Riviera," he pleaded in a loud voice.

Lauren shook with suppressed giggles.

"It's your line," he whispered into her ear before he began nibbling on it.

"I can't!" She choked with laughter. "I just can't!"

"Yes, you can!"

She gasped for breath and cried, "No, Renaldo! Father would kill us if he knew!"

He stepped back and clasped his forehead in mock anguish. "Then my life is as nothing! Fair maiden, you have destroyed a true and honest heart! I go now. Cyanide awaits me!"

And with a grand flourish, he was out the door.

Miss Emerson looked sternly at Lauren.

Lauren felt her face growing hot. She forced her mouth into a halfhearted smile and shrugged. "He's just mad about me," she said weakly.

Miss Emerson's mouth dropped open.

When she'd locked the door behind her, Lauren began giggling again.

CHAPTER FOURTEEN

Kobelski's book was still lying on the table. Lauren's light-hearted mood vanished. Who wanted to think about mass murder after such a great evening?

Still she had to do it. Her life might depend upon being able to recognize the murderer before his hands were at her throat.

She dressed for bed, then curled up on the sofa and began leafing through the book. Her heart sank in dismay. With the long unwieldy sentences heavy with medical terminology, it would take forever to get through the whole thing. But upon closer examination she realized that interspersed with the technical material were summaries of actual cases. Perhaps if she read those, she could grasp the salient points.

There was the case of the young man who shot ten people with a rifle from the top floor of an office building. He'd been an eagle scout, an honor student, a football star in high school and enormously popular. The community where he lived was shocked and bewildered. How could such a *nice* person— and from such a good home—do such a terrible thing?

Further investigation, however, revealed that the man's childhood had a dark side. Though his father appeared to be a pleasant, mild-mannered man, he had regularly beaten his wife and children for real or imagined misdeeds. The fact that his violence was kept a family secret added to the boy's problems. The pressure of living a lie had built up for years, gradually creating an enormous rage within the young man.

Shortly after he was imprisoned for his crimes, it was discovered that he had a small brain tumor which caused recurring dizzy spells. The author theorized that the tumor had caused a deterioration of the brain function so that the man's normal moral inhibitions could no longer hold him back from acting out his rage. The case was an example of a phenomenon known as displacement. That meant that the victims of his rage were not the cause of it.

Lauren looked up *displacement* in the index at the back of the book and found another case relating to it. A man had assaulted and killed five middle-aged women over a period of two years. After he was apprehended, it was discovered that each murder had taken place following a quarrel with his wife. It was also found that he'd been a victim of parental abuse as a child. He'd been taught to express frustration by brutality, the author explained.

There was the case of the friendless teenager who had knifed six strangers at various times before he was caught. He explained that God had commanded him to kill. He was found not guilty by reason of insanity and hospitalized for psychosis.

The physical description of the friendless young boy reminded Lauren of Paul. But Paul didn't hear voices, did he? He wasn't psychotic; he hadn't lost touch with reality. Or had he? He certainly did imagine that Lauren didn't like him. That she was deliberately making trouble for him. But that was paranoia, wasn't it? Seeing enemies where there were none?

She looked up paranoia and found the case of the young woman who shot four nurses because she imagined that her stillborn child had in reality been stolen and sold by an attending nurse.

Tired, and somewhat depressed, Lauren put the book down and yawned. They were all sad, sick lonely people. She didn't want to think about murder anymore.

There was a timid knock at the door.

"Who is it?"

"Jane Emerson, dearie!"

Lauren sighed with exasperation and looked at her watch. It was eleven-thirty. Didn't that old woman *ever* sleep? She unlocked the door.

Wrapped again in her lavender robe, Miss Emerson glanced around the apartment before speaking. "I forgot to tell you—that man was here again, looking for you."

Lauren was surprised. "Did he leave his name this time?"

Miss Emerson shook her head. "And I asked. *Twice*. But he wouldn't tell me. Most mysterious!"

"What did he say?"

Miss Emerson took a deep breath. "Well, I came out into the hall, and there he was, knocking on your door. I told him that you weren't in—that you'd gone out with your—er—young man." She looked pointedly at Lauren. "Er—Renaldo. He seemed upset about that."

Lauren was puzzled. Who could it be?

"He asked if I knew when you'd be back, and of course I said I had no idea. Then I said that if he would leave his name and telephone number, I would ask you to call him."

"And?"

"He didn't seem to like that idea at all. He said he'd keep trying to catch you at home. So I said, 'If you'll give me your name, I'll tell her that you were here.' And do you know what?" She paused expectantly.

"What?"

"He got *very* flustered. He said, 'Oh, no! I don't want you to do that!' "

Lauren frowned. "Was he tall or short?"

"Mm. Tallish."

"Light or dark?"

"Oh, dark."

Tallish and dark. Lauren was still puzzled. Paul was dark, but not very tall. And besides, Miss Emerson would have recognized him. Kobelski was tall, but not very dark. And yesterday Miss Emerson had described the caller as a young man. She looked at the little woman doubtfully. Maybe, at her age, Kobelski would be considered a "young man." But Kobelski wouldn't have been knocking on her door. He knew that she was going to dinner with Terry.

She shook her head. "I haven't the faintest idea who he

can be, Miss Emerson. And I certainly can't imagine what he wants. I guess I'll just have to wait a little longer."

The woman gave her a knowing look. "You certainly have your share of admirers, dearie! But I suppose that's only natural for a pretty girl like you."

Lauren suppressed a giggle as the tiny woman turned to leave. Paul had brought her home on Friday evening, Terry on Saturday and again tonight. She was sure that Miss Emerson had noticed Kobelski's coffee cup by the sink on Friday morning. And now some mysterious man was looking for her!

Later, as she laid out her clothes for the next morning, Lauren thought of Terry and smiled. It had been such a nice evening. And he did like her. There had been no awkward moments this evening—except that she'd lied so blatantly about her parents.

She never lied. It even bothered her to tell "little white lies" out of politeness. So why had she told Terry that her father was dead? And that her mother had managed to cope without leaning on her?

Because the truth hurt too damned much, that's why. She'd always resented her mother's dependence upon her, but before tonight, she'd never realized that she actually hated her mother for it. Hated her for being weak when she should have been strong. Hated her for not being there when Lauren needed her. For missing eighth-grade graduation because of a hangover. For bursting into tears of self-pity when Lauren brought her first date home to meet her mother, and for driving Lauren's father away.

That was the real reason for her hatred, wasn't it? If Ma hadn't been the kind of person she was, Lauren's father would never have left home. She had driven him away.

Lauren dropped the sweater she'd been folding as the image of her father came back to her with renewed clarity. She saw him standing in the center of the living room, his feet apart, his hat pushed to the back of his head. He was laughing. He had a hearty laugh that made her glow. Yes, that was her father. Funny how she'd forgotten the dark lock of hair tumbling across his forehead. But she'd been so young when he left.

One thing she knew for sure. He was a gentle man. He'd held her on his lap. Had he read her stories? She wasn't certain. She tried to picture his hands. They were big, certainly. Such a tall man must have big hands. And long fingers, like a pianist's.

She sat down on the edge of her bed. Maybe that was what "on the road" meant. Maybe her father had been a musician. That would fit in another way, too. How could a man with a sensitive artistic temperament live with a woman like Ma? He'd had to go away. If it hadn't been for Ma. . .

Suddenly Lauren was nine years old, standing beside Aunt Lil in the old living room. She could see the dark green wallpaper with large white flowers. Through the window came the red flash of ambulance lights.

"I only hope it's not too late," Aunt Lil was saying sourly.

"I hope it is," thought young Lauren. "I hope she dies."

She had just finished reading *Sensible Kate*. Young orphaned Kate had finally been adopted by a lovely couple who were such fun. Perhaps if she were an orphan, someone nice would adopt her, and she would live happily ever after.

Lauren started. Had she really felt like that as a little girl? Had she hated Ma even way back then?

She caught herself. Didn't all children think they hated their parents occasionally? There was no sense blaming Ma for everything. She had her good points. She'd always worked steadily at a monotonous job in the book bindery, and she never spent much on herself. Lauren came first. And even during the periods when she was drinking, she'd been a passive kind of problem. She simply drank until she fell asleep. She'd never been abusive or cruel.

And when she wasn't drinking—which was really most of the time—she'd encouraged Lauren, helped with her homework, always made sure her school dresses were freshly pressed. And how she'd fussed with Lauren's hair, brushing it a hundred strokes every evening and tying it with a bright ribbon in the morning.

Ma didn't know how to be close to her daughter, but she had tried. Poor Ma! Lauren could see her. The eyes that always looked away in shame, the once-pretty face now lined with anxiety and fatigue. Poor Ma! She just wasn't strong. But it wasn't a crime not to be strong.

With a sudden rush of shame, Lauren remembered the hatred she'd felt toward her mother only moments before. All those years of stored-up resentment. Was she so different from those people she'd been reading about? People who killed?

Lauren shivered. Human emotions were awfully complex.

CHAPTER FIFTEEN

Warren Bell wore a European-tailored shirt and coordinated slacks to class on Monday. A gold chain circled his throat above the wisps of hair which poked through his unbuttoned collar.

"Today's lecture will deal with cellular membranes," he said, speaking in a voice as carefully modulated as a trained actor's. "It is all too easy to dismiss the membrane as simply the boundary of the cell. In fact, however, the membrane plays an important role in the cell's daily life. This is so chiefly because the membrane is *permeable*."

He paused to write the word *permeable* on the chalkboard.

"Permeable means that dissolved matter is allowed to pass through the membrane. Thus, the cell can acquire nutrients and dispose of waste products."

He paused again and began to draw a diagram in colored chalk on the board, explaining as he drew. His diagrams were always large, vivid and clearly labeled. At the same time, they were simple enough to be easily copied into notebooks without confusion. "Natural unit membranes have a kind of 'sandwich' structure," he was saying.

When the bell sounded at the end of the hour, he rapped on the podium for attention. "I'd like to remind you that Wednesday there will be an hour examination. It will cover the material from the first six chapters of your text as well as the supplementary material on cytogenetics."

As Lauren picked up her notes, Nedra Hines edged up to her. "How did the 'conference' go on Saturday?"

"Not bad," Lauren answered. "I really did have trouble with that quiz, even though I hadn't realized it."

115

"Did he ask you out?"

"Not in so many words, but I think the invitation was there, between the lines."

"How did you handle it?"

"I turned him down."

"Good for you."

"But I've changed my mind."

"*What?*" Nedra looked at her with disbelief. "Boy, I sure hope you know what you're doing!"

So do I, Lauren thought.

She approached Bell at the beginning of the laboratory session. He was handing out mimeographed sheets with instructions for their next experiment. She waited until he had distributed all of them. "Professor Bell?"

He turned to her with a flicker of surprise in his eyes. "Yes?"

"I—I've given some thought to what you said—about my work. Perhaps I do need some help. Just to make sure I'm on the right track."

He seemed pleased. "I'll do my best to help you."

And what does that mean? Lauren wondered. "Do you suppose—one evening this week?" she asked.

"Certainly. Are you free tonight? We could discuss things over dinner."

"I have to work tonight," Lauren said.

"Too bad. It would have been nice to get in a session before Wednesday's exam. But I imagine you'll do all right in that. It's strictly an objective test. How about dinner on Thursday evening?"

"That will be fine."

He gave her hand a little squeeze. "Yes, it will be. Just fine."

Lauren's heart sank. *Boy, Kobelski,* she thought, *you're really getting me into a fix! How am I going to wriggle out of this situation and still get a decent grade?*

She went to her microscope and began examining the slides she had prepared in last Friday's class. With a sense of wonder she surveyed the small world beneath the microscope lens. All those tiny details. She frowned. What was that pink area? It shouldn't be there.

Bell came up behind her and put his hands on her shoulders. "How are we doing?" His manner was overly solicitous.

Embarrassed, Lauren moved away from the microscope to let him have a look.

"This is very nice," he said, squinting into the eyepiece. "You managed to get good contrast. But there, in the lower left quadrant—the slightly reddish area. Do you know what that is?"

Lauren squirmed uneasily. "No, I—I don't." Another chance for him to lower her grade.

But he smiled warmly at her. "You didn't quite remove all the excess red dye when you stained your sample. That's all. It's a good idea to always use one more rinse than you think you'll need."

He looked through the other slides she had prepared. "You're doing fine," he said, moving away. "Keep up the good work."

Lauren wondered whether his reaction would have been so genial if she hadn't agreed to meet with him on Thursday. She looked at him. He was now bending over another girl, his hand resting on her arm, his face brushing her hair as he looked over her shoulder into her microscope.

From across the room, Nedra gave her an "I told you so" look.

By the time Lauren left the building, the skies had opened up and produced a downpour. Lauren hadn't worn a raincoat or carried her umbrella, so she stood in the entrance waiting for the shuttle bus that would take her back to Area 17. But in the dash from the entrance to the bus, she got soaked to the skin, so once in her car, she headed for her apartment to change into dry clothes. She'd be a little late for work, but she couldn't very well work all day in wet clothes.

She parked her car and dashed to the entrance of the building. Miss Emerson was standing in the doorway to her apartment, talking with a young man. Apparently he had been there for a while, for Lauren noticed that his tennis shoes and jeans were completely dry. He turned as she came in.

With a start, Lauren recognized him as the fellow with the long narrow face who had been watching her so intently in the Nite Owl last Saturday.

When he saw her, he flushed and looked away.

Miss Emerson, however, piped up cheerfully. "Oh, hello, Lauren. I don't believe you've met my nephew, Andrew Neely. Andrew, this is Miss Walker."

"How do you do," the young man mumbled like a bashful child. His eyes avoided Lauren's. He turned back to Miss Emerson. "I really must go, Aunt Jane." He started for the door. "Nice meeting you, Miss Walker."

Why was he so uneasy? Lauren wondered.

When he had gone, Miss Emerson looked at her steadily. "Such a shy boy! He's really a dear, but terribly reserved." She paused. "I'll admit he's not much on looks—takes after his father—but he's very serious. Not like some young men are these days!"

Lauren suppressed a smile. Terry's performance last night had obviously made an unfavorable impression on Miss Emerson and she felt duty-bound to let Lauren know.

"I think I've met your nephew before," Lauren said casually. "Is he a student?"

To her surprise, Miss Emerson seemed somewhat taken aback by the question. "Why, I think he is taking a course at the university this semester," she said rather haltingly. "Is that where you've seen him?"

The question was asked in a slightly sharper tone. Evidently she kept a watchful eye on her nephew, Lauren thought. She was a busybody!

Instantly, Lauren sympathized with Andrew. She wasn't going to tell Miss Emerson that she'd seen him in a bar. Old eagle-eye would probably disapprove and give the poor kid a hard time. "I think I've seen him on campus. I'm not sure," she said. "Would he be taking a course in the Life Sciences Building?"

An amused glint came into Miss Emerson's eyes. "Maybe. I'm not sure." She matched Lauren's inflections exactly.

She knows I'm not leveling with her, Lauren thought. *Wouldn't she be a terror to live with!*

"You should get out of those wet clothes before you catch pneumonia, dearie."

Relieved at the opportunity to end the conversation, Lauren agreed.

She was a half hour late to work. Dr. Herbert was in the lab and he was obviously angry.

"I'm sorry for being late," Lauren apologized as she hung up her raincoat and put her umbrella in the storage room to dry. She really hadn't expected him to be upset. "I had to go home and change clothes—I got caught in the rain."

"Oh, it's not you, my dear," he said quickly. "It's Paul."

Poor Paul! In trouble again. "What did he do?"

"It's what he *didn't* do. He didn't come to work today!"

"Perhaps he's ill," Lauren suggested as she put on her lab coat.

"If so, he should have called," Dr. Herbert snapped. "Look! Fifty samples from Bethesda were delivered this morning. The fool messenger found no one here so he simply left the box in the hall. Those samples have been unrefrigerated all morning!"

There was nothing Lauren could say. She closed her eyes in exasperation. How did Paul expect her to put in a good word for him when he behaved so irresponsibly?

"What's more," Dr. Herbert went on, "I need the results of the tests he did two weeks ago on the samples from Atlanta. He was supposed to have them ready for me. I can't find them anywhere."

"Have you looked through his notes?" Lauren asked.

"That's the trouble! I have. Look at this mess!"

Lauren looked over his shoulder. The first rule of a good scientist was to keep careful notes on every step of an experiment, so that it could be duplicated, when necessary, by anyone reading the notes. Paul's entries, however, were not even legible.

"Do you suppose this is a four or a seven?" Dr. Herbert demanded, pointing to a carelessly formed digit on one of the test sheets. "And look here! You can't even read where these samples are from!"

Lauren looked at the date on the test sheet. "Last Monday. Those are the samples from Des Moines."

Dr. Herbert shook his head. "A month from now, one might not be so sure of that. Paul is simply falling apart! These last few weeks—it's as if he's in a daze! I don't know what's the matter with him."

"But you *do* think it's come on rather suddenly, don't you?" Lauren asked.

Dr. Herbert looked at her over the top of his rimless glasses. "Oh, yes. You can even tell it by looking at his notes. Here! A month ago." He flipped the pages of Paul's notebook. "Look how neat it is. Everything filled in. Everything legible. But here"—he flipped forward several sheets—"three weeks ago. Notice how much harder it is to read the numbers?"

Three weeks ago, Lauren thought. Shortly after Ellen's death. Had there been a similar pattern after Dee Dee's murder? Casually she thumbed back through Paul's notes until she came to the tests done in the middle of July. But there was nothing obviously wrong there. If Paul had been disturbed after Diane Towle's death, it didn't show in his work.

Where did that leave things? Paul had known Ellen. His picture in her sketchbook was mute testimony to that fact. Had he known her fairly well? Was that why he had been upset since her murder? Or was there something more?

"And now these samples won't be tested today," Dr. Herbert said petulantly.

"I can do some of them today and some more tomorrow," Lauren said. "If you need the data, you'll have it by Friday." He didn't need it, she knew. He was just blowing off steam now and looking for any excuse to be angrier with Paul.

What *had* happened to Paul? Lauren found herself wondering about him as she carefully added the reagents, drop by drop, to the appropriate test tubes. There was no excuse for his not calling to explain his absence. Especially after he'd asked her to intercede with Dr. Herbert for him.

As soon as she had set up her own tests, Lauren began to prepare Paul's samples for testing. She examined the samples critically. Going without refrigeration that morning hadn't caused much lysis of the red cells. The plasma was still clear to the eye. But it was another variable—an unnecessary one—in the experimental procedure. That, she knew, was what had really bothered Dr. Herbert. And it was also something that Paul wouldn't understand.

She had barely finished setting up Paul's test when a desk timer rang, reminding her to read the results of her own tests. She discovered, too, that she needed to prepare fresh starch gels for the electrophoretic tests she'd have to run tomorrow. Damn! Doing Paul's work was really setting her back. Why did she feel so responsible for him? she wondered. Why not let him solve his own problems?

But she wouldn't. She'd always help him. She knew that. There was something in Paul that brought out strong protective feelings in her.

It was nearly ten when Lauren finally got home. She half expected Miss Emerson to be watching for her, but there was no sign of the old woman as she entered the building.

It was funny, she thought, as she took an orange from the refrigerator, that she felt so differently about Miss Emerson at different times. Sometimes she seemed like a sweet little woman who only wanted to help even when her help wasn't needed—or wanted. At other times she seemed like a nosy old bag. Well, maybe that was a bit strong. But Lauren had felt an intense dislike for her when she started prying into her nephew's affairs. It wasn't really anything Miss Emerson had said. It was her manner. Maybe it was all in Lauren's mind. One of those mental triggers that Kobelski talked about. Maybe Miss Emerson reminded her of Ma: "Where are you going *now?* You're *always* leaving me alone! You're late! You *know* I worry when you're late!''

Lauren tossed the peels into the garbage. That was probably it. Miss Emerson's questions about Andrew had annoyed her so much because they reminded her of Ma.

Funny how the mind worked. Funny, too, how the fellow who'd been watching her at the Nite Owl turned out to be Miss Emerson's nephew. Life was full of coincidences.

Someone rapped on her door.

''Who is it?''

''Lauren, I've got to talk to you.''

It was the last voice on earth she'd expected to hear.

She opened the door.

He was a good head taller than she. He wore an expensively tailored business suit in a rich brown which seemed to have been chosen especially to emphasize his dark eyes and coloring. His hair was freshly trimmed.

Lauren's heart quickened. He looked exactly as she remembered him.

He gave her a forced smile. ''Aren't you even going to say hello?''

She swallowed. ''Hello, Doug.''

CHAPTER SIXTEEN

For a moment they stood staring at each other. Then he said softly, "You could invite me in."

Lauren was flustered. "Yes, of course. I'm sorry."

As she showed him into the living room, she glanced involuntarily at his left hand. The third finger was bare. A thin band of untanned skin showed that he had recently worn a ring.

"Well" she said in a too bright voice. "How are you?"

"Fine." He settled back in his chair. "Dad promoted me to head of marketing. It's a really interesting position. I travel most of the time now." He looked at her. "You've changed your hair, I see. It looks nice."

"Thank you."

There was an uncomfortable silence. How unreal it seemed, she thought. She had once thought of marrying this man, and now here they were, struggling to make small talk.

He cleared his throat. "How do you like graduate school?"

"I like it a lot." She wondered if he believed her. He had never understood her desire for further education.

With one well-manicured finger, Doug absently picked at a worn spot on the arm of the sofa. He looked around the room. It seemed to Lauren that his very presence made everything seem even shabbier than usual. "So this is where you live," he said softly.

Lauren detected the faintest catch in his voice and knew what he was thinking. *Would life with me have been so unpleasant that you prefer to live like this?*

He would never understand, she thought with a pang.

"Can I make you some coffee?"

He shook his head. "My doctor warned me to lay off the stuff. I seem to be getting an ulcer. Can you imagine that? An ulcer at my age?"

"Maybe you're working too hard," she suggested.

He looked away. "No, it's not that. It's——" He didn't finish.

An awkward silence hung between them.

Finally, Lauren asked, "Were you here yesterday?"

He looked at her uncomfortably. "Yeah. And the night before, too. Actually, I was supposed to be in Bloomington today, but I stayed over because I wanted to see you."

Lauren felt a tightening in her chest. "How's Nancy?" she asked pointedly.

"Unhappy. We both are." He glanced at his left hand. "She's filed for divorce," he said bluntly.

Lauren was stunned. "Oh, Doug! I'm sorry."

"I made a terrible mistake, Lauren." The words came out in a sudden rush. "When you—when you broke our engagement, I—well, it hurt. I felt I'd been humiliated in front of my family and friends." He paused and swallowed. "I wanted to hurt you in return. That's why I married Nancy."

Lauren stared silently at him. This was a different Douglas Martin. Not quite as smooth and self-assured as before.

"Sometimes counseling——" she suggested.

He shook his head. "We tried that. It's no good. The whole thing was a mistake from the beginning. We couldn't seem to agree on anything, what kind of furniture to buy, which friends to ask over, where to go for dinner. We were always pulling in different directions. It got so I hated to go home at night. Finally, I just didn't. You can't imagine the hell I've been through!" He leaned forward, closer to her. "It would have been different with us, Lauren—you and me."

"Doug," Lauren protested, but she couldn't stop him.

"It's true. I was a fool. I used to think that having a working wife"— He shook his head—"I just couldn't see it." He looked at her anxiously. "But I should have understood. So what if you wanted to continue your education? Or have a career? We could have managed. Even if we had children——"

"Doug, I don't think you should be saying these things."

He gave her a pained look. "I've spent nearly six weeks getting up the courage. I've got to tell you."

Lauren felt Doug's old power drawing her in again. She had to keep her head, to be careful of her words. She'd been hurt—terribly hurt—before. And, evidently, so had he. She got up and walked to the window, her face turned away from his. "Please Doug," she said carefully. "I want you to leave."

"Not until I've said what I came here to say." He stood up, came over to her and took her in his arms. "I want you, Lauren." His voice was heavy, pleading. "I've always loved you, and I shouldn't have let you leave me."

For all his sophistication, there was something disarmingly boyish about Doug. It was easy to understand why his parents had always indulged him. It was difficult to refuse him anything, especially when he looked at you with those brown eyes softly pleading. Lauren had always felt a strong physical attraction toward Doug. Now, with his arms around her, she was tempted to close her eyes and let him hold her close, to kiss her, to——

She was surprised at the depth of her feelings. She'd thought that everything between her and Doug was over. She'd been fooling herself.

"I know you still have some feeling for me," he said, searching her face.

He bent forward to kiss her, but she pulled away. "No, Doug, please!"

He smiled. "Everything aboveboard, huh? You always were that way. Okay!" He backed away. "I'll keep my hands off. I won't even see you without a chaperone until the divorce is final. I just want to know that you'll be here, waiting for me."

She shook her head. "It's no good, Doug. Your parents didn't approve of me before. Now——"

"Now they'll see that I was right in the first place. They.

approved of Nancy, you know. And they saw what a disaster that marriage was!''

"But it still won't work.''

"Don't say that! We haven't given it a chance.''

She searched for words. "Doug, I've changed.''

"I can see that.'' He looked at her appreciatively. "And I like it.''

"That isn't what I meant. I mean I've changed as a person.''

His face suddenly darkened. "Is there another man?''

Lauren hesitated. She couldn't say that she was in love with Terry. That would be putting it too strongly. How could she be in love with someone she'd only met a couple of days ago?

Still . . . "I have met someone.''

"But there's still a chance for me, isn't there?'' Doug looked at her hopefully.

She sighed. "Doug, I——''

He held up his hand. "You don't have to answer me now. I know this is sudden. Just think about it, okay? I'm in town every weekend.''

"Every weekend?''

"Sure. I took an apartment here last July when Nancy and I decided to separate. It's central to my sales territory. No sense in driving up to Waterville every weekend. There's nothing there for me now.'' His voice thickened at the last sentence.

"You've been here all this time?'' Lauren looked at him, surprised.

"Well, weekends, anyhow. You can imagine how I felt when I heard that you were here at school. I've been trying to get up the nerve to see you. He gave a little nervous laugh and looked at the floor. "Then when I finally did come, I found that you'd gone out with someone else two evenings in a row. I nearly gave up.''

"You could have called first.''

He shook his head. "Would you have let me come here if I had?''

"Probably not."

"You see! I still know you pretty well, don't I?"

Lauren looked at him helplessly.

He smiled. "You may have changed the way you look, but you haven't changed inside, have you?"

She turned away.

"Look," he said uncomfortably, "it won't be long. Dad's lawyers are drawing up the settlement. It's very generous. Nancy will get the house, a car, a nice sum of cash."

The disposable wife, Lauren thought.

He caught the pained look on her face. "You don't understand! *She* wants the divorce, too! She'll be happy to accept a good settlement."

"Stop it, Doug!"

He shrugged. "It sounds awful, doesn't it? But please understand, Lauren. It was never really a marriage. Just a sad imitation. Nancy and I both agreed that it was a foolish, impulsive mistake." He looked at her pleadingly. "You wouldn't hold a mistake against me, would you?"

"I'm not holding anything against you."

"Then give me a chance to start over. And this time it'll be different, Lauren."

"Will it?" She felt misgivings. "You always had such definite ideas, Doug. What happens when we disagree again?"

"We won't disagree! You'll see!" His face was flushed. "You can have anything you want."

"But I don't——"

"No decisions now," he interrupted. "Think about it. I'll be back in town on Friday night. What time can I see you?"

She thought for a moment. "I work until nine on Fridays."

He smiled. "I'll be here at ten."

Lauren lay in bed, sleepless. Why now? Of all times for Doug to reappear! If he had come to her a year ago and said he'd had a change of heart, she'd have been overjoyed. Now she felt only confusion. Doug's parents had always overindulged him. He'd always gotten whatever he wanted—until she'd broken their engagement. Was she, in a way, responsible for his disastrous marriage? Perhaps if she had let him down easier. . . .

She turned her pillow over and pressed her burning cheek to the cool side. What was she going to do this time? She still loved him.

Doug sometimes had an uncanny knack of knowing how her mind worked. He'd known that if she saw him again, if he held her in his arms again, she wouldn't be able to lie to herself. And he'd been right.

But if she loved him and if he truly had changed his mind about her career, why did she hesitate? What was keeping her from saying yes?

CHAPTER SEVENTEEN

When Lauren arrived at work on Tuesday morning, she felt tired and irritable. She'd gotten very little sleep after Doug left.

She found Paul in a black mood. He was placing several test tubes into a centrifuge. In reply to her greeting, he angrily banged down the lid of the machine. Lauren clenched her teeth. It pained her to see laboratory equipment abused.

"What's eating you?" she asked, trying to keep her voice free of the irritation she felt. "I'm the one who ought to be angry. I ended up doing half your work yesterday, and you didn't even have the decency to call and explain why you weren't coming in."

"Who told you to do my tests?" Paul snapped as he started up the centrifuge. As it spun faster and faster, it emitted a high-pitched whine.

Lauren was taken aback. "Why, no one *told* me to. I just thought I'd——"

"You just thought you'd pick up a few more brownie points with Dr. Herbert and make me look that much worse!" He picked up a sheet of paper which had been lying on the worktable, crumpled it into a ball and hurled it toward the wastebasket, missing his mark widely.

"Paul, why didn't you come to work yesterday?"

He frowned so that his dark brows almost met. "I couldn't. I had to think—to figure out what was going on."

"What do you mean?"

He looked at her with narrowed eyes. "You know! You're part of it! You said you weren't, but you have to be! Changing your hair—looking like——"

Lauren shook her head impatiently. "Paul, I told you——"

"I know what you told me, and I almost believed you. I even thought you might help me."

She was unable to contain herself. "And I wanted to! But how am I supposed to put in a good word for you when you act the way you did yesterday?"

For a moment he looked contrite. "I'm sorry. I didn't think. I was so mixed up."

"It would help if you explained to me what you're so mixed up about."

"You seem to be on my side sometimes," he said slowly.

"Of course I'm on your side." Lauren's head was beginning to throb.

"No, you have to be one of them."

She stared at him. Talk about paranoia! She was one of *them* again! She pulled a stool out from beneath the workbench and sat down. "Paul," she said slowly. "Who are *they?*"

"The police, of course!" He began to pace back and forth. "They're saying things about me that aren't true! They think I'm crazy!" He lowered his face to hers. Perspiration glistened on his forehead. *"I'm not crazy!"* He seemed to shrink into himself and his voice became very small. "I'm afraid."

"I think I understand," Lauren said, taking one of his hands in hers. "This is about Ellen Rickover, isn't it?"

At the mention of the girl's name, Paul pulled his hand away as if it had been burned.

"I didn't kill her," he said quickly. "I didn't even know her. I just—I met her on campus one day last summer. I was going to talk to the dean about being admitted as a special student." His words tumbled out rapidly. He seemed short of breath. "She—she said she wanted to do a sketch of my face. She thought it had interesting lines. I sat on the ledge of the fountain. Fifteen minutes, maybe. That's all."

"Did you like her?" Lauren asked.

Paul shrugged. "She was just a girl who wanted to draw my face."

"Didn't you think she was—well, pretty?"

"I guess so," he said indifferently.

She hesitated. "Did she remind you of anyone?"

He frowned. "No. I mean, she looked like you, but I didn't know you then."

"Tell me about your family." Lauren said in what she hoped was a casual manner. "What's your mother like?"

Paul's expression underwent a subtle change. "Like any mother, I guess."

"I take it you aren't very close."

He seemed confused. "I don't know what you mean. Of course we're close. I love my mother, just like everybody else. What does that have to do with anything?"

Lauren looked at him uncertainly and decided not to pursue the matter. "Nothing, really," she said gently. "Let's talk about Ellen."

"There's nothing to talk about. I never saw her again."

"Weren't you upset when you read in the papers that she'd been murdered?"

"No." Paul shook his head. "I didn't even remember her when I read about the—the murder. I didn't know it was the same girl."

He took a deep breath. "Then the police came. They kept asking questions. They said I'd gone to her apartment, hadn't I?" That I'd killed her, hadn't I?" Paul's voice was rising steadily. "But it wasn't true, any of it!" He took a deep breath and his voice became steadier. "They came back to question me again. And just when I thought that it was over and that they were going to leave me alone"—he looked at her—"*you* came here, looking like *that!*"

Lauren gasped. No wonder the change in her appearance had upset Paul. "But I didn't mean—that has nothing to do with the police questioning you."

Paul flushed. "Do you think I'm so stupid——"

"Paul, I would like to speak with you." Dr. Herbert stood in the doorway of the laboratory. His normally cheerful countenance looked grim; the lines on either side of his mouth were deep and rigid.

Lauren stood up quickly. "Dr. Herbert, perhaps I could speak with you first?"

He waved her away. "Paul?"

Meekly, Paul followed Dr. Herbert into the office on the other side of the hall.

Lauren's heart sank. If only she'd had a chance to speak to Dr. Herbert first and explain to him why Paul was upset. It was perfectly understandable why his work had fallen off lately. All she could do was hope that he wouldn't be too hard on Paul.

And yet, argued the little voice in the back of her mind, wasn't Paul overreacting? There must be hundreds of men in the city who had been questioned about the murders. They weren't all going to pieces, were they? But Paul was different, she told herself. He was kind of—fragile. Couldn't take a lot of stress.

He snaps, the little voice suggested. Didn't Kobelski say the killer might be someone like that?

The door to Dr. Herbert's office opened and Paul came out, his face dark with fury.

"I hope you're satisfied!" he hissed. "He fired me. And it's all your fault!"

"Oh, no! He can't do that!" She got up from her chair. "I'll tell him. I'll explain——"

Paul pushed her back into the chair. His eyes glittered with anger. "You've done enough already! Playing up to him, making me look incompetent! I won't forget that! And the way you made yourself look like *her*! I won't forget that, either!"

"Paul! Wait!" Lauren pleaded.

He tore off his lab coat and threw it to the floor. Halfway out the door, he turned and looked back at her with hatred.

"You'll pay for this!"

CHAPTER EIGHTEEN

Lauren was shaken. Paul had been angry before, but he had never acted like this! What did he mean, she would pay? Although his threat frightened her, she couldn't help feeling—as always where Paul was concerned—protective. Paul's behavior did make sense, considering all the things that had happened. His nervousness and fear had impaired his ability to think and work. When he saw her looking so much like Ellen, it was the last straw. Perhaps if she explained the circumstances to Dr. Herbert, he'd reconsider. Lauren crossed the hall to his office. But Dr. Herbert had already left for his regular Tuesday meeting with the finance committee. She would have to wait until later.

She began setting up one series of electrophoretic tests on the Bethesda samples. All blood samples were routinely tested for half a dozen different enzymes. She put the samples into a sheet of starch gel, then turned on the electric current which would be allowed to pass through it for several hours. This caused the enzymes to migrate through the gel. Because of their different weights and electrical charges, the enzymes migrated varying distances. Later, she'd assess the distance each sample traveled during a given period of time by comparing them to known standards. In this way, it was possible to identify the various enzymes present in the blood. The catch was that each enzyme test required a particular type of gel and a particular voltage. Even the temperature at which the tests were run varied. Everything had to be checked, double-checked, and recorded.

It was tiring to do a large number of tests in one day. Lauren decided to set up all the tests which were to be run at zero degrees centigrade. She did some calculating. She would need seventeen hours of electrical current. She sighed. Paul wouldn't be here tomorrow morning to turn it off, and she couldn't come in at nine because she had an exam.

Lauren looked at her watch. If she had everything prepared to begin the run by three-thirty this afternoon, she'd have time to stop in at the lab before going to class. But that would be cutting it very close. And it wasn't a good idea to rush when there were so many details to be checked. Better take her time, work late and get the whole thing started at eight in the evening. Then she could stop the run when she came in at her regular time at one o'clock the next afternoon.

Dr. Herbert did not return to the lab. Lauren checked with the department secretary and was informed that he was scheduled to give a speech in Milwaukee that evening. Talking with him about Paul would have to be postponed until tomorrow.

By eight o'clock she was ready. She had prepared each gel with its own particular buffer solutions. All the electrical connections were secure. Each power pack was set to the appropriate voltage. She checked the cold-room thermostat one last time and attached it to the automatic temperature recorder. If the refrigeration should accidentally be cut off during the night, the recorder would indicate how much the temperature of the room had been affected. All that remained to be done was to switch on the power packs.

Lauren was tired. It had been a long day, and the number of details to be checked had seemed endless.

It was eight-thirty when she got back to her apartment building. In the foyer, beside her door, stood a huge vase of long-stemmed yellow roses, at least two dozen. She knew even before she read the card that they were from Doug. Who else would be so extravagant?

The card said simply, "Consider." It was unsigned. Lauren crumpled it and put it into her coat pocket. What should she do with the flowers? She didn't want them. They evoked Doug's presence too powerfully. She couldn't make an objective decision while he seemed to be there with her. She needed to put some emotional distance between them. She looked over at Miss Emerson's door. *Why not?*

"Would you like these flowers?" she asked when the little woman opened the door. "A friend sent them, and I—uh—I'm allergic to roses."

Miss Emerson looked at her sharply. "They're lovely," she said slowly. "Are you sure you want to give them away?"

"Positive," Lauren said. She started to say more about her allergy, but Miss Emerson's bright eyes were watching her face closely. "I'm positive," she repeated.

"In that case," the old woman said, "I'll be happy to take them. Thank you very much."

Lauren smiled to herself as she unlocked her apartment door. It wasn't surprising that Miss Emerson had never married, she thought. Who'd want to live with someone who had a built-in lie detector?

As she hung up her coat, she suddenly had the uncomfortable feeling that something was wrong. Slowly she backed away from the closet and looked around the room.

Nothing was out of place. Cautiously, she went to the door of the bathroom and threw it open. Nothing there. Nor was anything disturbed in the bedroom. Even her hastily made bed was just as she'd left it, with her nightgown thrown across the pillow.

Why did she feel so uneasy? *You're tired*, she told herself. *And hungry.*

Rummaging in the cupboard, she found a can of pea soup. She warmed it up, diluting it only half as much as the directions recommended. Then she spread out her books on the kitchen table and began to read while she ate.

It was hard to concentrate. As soon as she managed to put Doug out of her mind, she found herself remembering the look in Paul's eyes. She shivered. Was she really frightened of Paul, or had all those hours in the cold room given her a chill?

When she realized that she had read the same page three times without knowing what it said she closed the book. Although it was only a little after nine, she decided she would not try to study any more tonight. She'd get up early and start fresh tomorrow.

The phone rang.

"I can't figure it out. You've got my number and yet you never call me. Is my irresistible charm wearing thin?"

"Terry! How good to hear you."

"What are you doing?"

Lauren groaned. "Trying to absorb enough cytology to get a good grade on the exam tomorrow."

"Oh! A toughie, huh?"

"That's just the trouble. I don't know. Until a couple of days ago, I thought I had the subject down cold. Now I'm afraid that an in-depth question could stump me completely."

"Would you like a magic spell to solve the problem?"

"A WHAT?"

"Repeat slowly after me: I will ace this exam. I can do anything because Terry cares about me."

Lauren swallowed. "Do you?"

"Mmm, you bet. That spell is reserved for angels, fairy princesses, and true loves."

Lauren wasn't sure how to react. "I guess that puts me in pretty good company," she said, hoping her voice sounded light and amused.

"Actually, it was my company I wanted to put you in. But if you've got an exam tomorrow . . ."

"I'm sorry," she said honestly, "but I still have another chapter to review and I have to get some sleep. I've had a hard day."

"In that case, I'll let you take a rain check. How about Saturday night? We're having a party here at the apartment. A little music, a little cheese and crackers, a lot of beer."

Lauren laughed. "Sounds like fun."

She hung up feeling considerably more cheerful. And awake. Maybe she'd polish off the last chapter tonight after all. She'd sleep better, knowing it was done. She began to study in earnest.

It was nearly eleven when, on impulse, she pushed the shade of the front window aside and looked out. There was a figure in the shadows across the street. She turned away from the window, feeling reassured. Kobelski was on the job.

Then she stopped. That figure didn't look like Kobelski.

She turned off the lights in order to have a better look without being conspicuous. From the darkness of her living room, she looked out again. This time she was sure. It *wasn't* Kobelski. This man wasn't tall enough. And even if she had misjudged his height at this distance, his shoulders certainly weren't as broad as the detective's.

For a moment, she thought of Paul, and the memory of the hate-filled look he'd given her as he left the lab. Maybe it was Paul across the street. It was hard to judge from this distance and in this bad light. But if it were Paul, why was he there? She remembered suddenly that the last words he had spoken to her were, "You'll pay for this!"

She stepped away from the window again, shaking.

Take it easy, she told herself. *Whoever's out there, Kobelski's got his eye on him. He'll make sure you're okay.*

On the other hand, she thought, it wouldn't hurt to look out for herself a bit. She took one of the chairs from the kitchenette and propped it under the doorknob. No matter how silently someone might pick the lock, any movement of the door itself would cause the chair legs to grate noisily across the floor.

She raided the kitchen cabinets, the bathroom, and the top of her bureau, gathering drinking glasses and bottles of makeup, cologne, shampoo, and face cream, and lined them up along each windowsill. Any movement of the shades would send them crashing to the hardwood floor.

There! Now let anyone try to get in without her knowing it!

A little doubt still assailed her, however, and she decided to keep a weapon at her bedside, just in case. A knife under the pillow. But when she opened the kitchen drawer, she remembered that Kobelski had taken all her knives. He'd taken her scissors and her skewer, too.

That worked both ways, didn't it? For a moment, she felt panic. Why didn't it occur to him that *she* might need a weapon?

She tried to think. There had to be something in the apartment that she could use. She tried a frying pan for weight. Too clumsy. She finally fell into a troubled sleep clutching her steam iron.

CHAPTER NINETEEN

Lauren quickly looked over the exam. How did Remak's and Virchov's ideas contribute to the support of Darwin's theory of evolution? Easy. She knew that one. Sutton's chromosomal theory of inheritance? She'd anticipated that question. So far, so good. Structure and function of ribosomes? Endoplasmic reticulum. Mitochondria. ATP.

By the time she'd scanned all the questions, Lauren felt confident. The questions were straightforward.

She wrote quickly, answering each question in as much detail as possible. By the time the bell rang at the end of the hour, she had rechecked each of her answers and felt satisfied.

Professor Bell was standing by the door of the lecture hall, collecting the exams as the students filed out. When he saw Lauren, he smiled. "What did you think of it?"

"I thought it was a very fair exam," she answered. "It covered a little of everything, and the questions didn't seem ambiguous."

He looked pleased. "I'm sure you did just fine. Oh, by the way, about tomorrow night—seven o'clock in the faculty dining room all right?"

Heads turned and Lauren flushed. She wished he hadn't said that in front of the other students. She nodded and hurried on to the laboratory session.

As she unlocked the cabinet containing her laboratory equipment, Nedra Hines came over to her. "I couldn't help overhearing," she whispered. "You weren't kidding! You're really going out with him?"

Lauren felt a surge of impatience. "I'm going to have dinner with him—in a public place—to discuss how I botched my last quiz and how I can avoid doing it again.''

"*Sure* you are.''

Lauren frowned. "You know, Nedra, I'm not entirely sure that he's such a bad guy. He is a good teacher and he honestly seems to want to help me.''

"You and a dozen other girls,'' Nedra sniffed.

Lauren flushed. "Just the same, I'm reserving judgment on him.''

The small dark girl shrugged. "Well, there's something you'd better know before you do anything.''

Lauren closed the cabinet door and removed the cover from a new box of slides. "What are you talking about?''

"He's divorced, you know.''

"Lots of people are,'' Lauren said impatiently.

"Yes, I know, but his wife got everything. The house, the car, the savings account—everything. She cleaned him out.''

Lauren felt suddenly tired. "Nedra, I'm going to spend a couple of hours with him talking about my work! I have no interest in him, romantic or otherwise, and I couldn't care less about his financial condition!''

"That's not what I mean.'' Nedra looked around to be sure no one else was listening. "I heard she filed for divorce because he beat her. The university let him know that if anything unsavory was revealed in court, he would be out of a job.''

Lauren stared at her.

"Don't you see?'' Nedra went on. "He bought her off! He had to give her everything he had to keep her quiet.''

It must have been very painful for him, Lauren thought. Just from the clothes he wore, it was plain to see that Warren Bell liked money. If she had taken him financially, he must hate his wife. "Do you know what she looked like?'' she asked.

"His wife? I saw her once. Good looking, blonde——''

From behind them, Professor Bell said, "Nedra, may I see you for a couple of minutes?''

Lauren bent over her slides, her face hot. Had he overheard enough to know they'd been talking about him?

Nothing in his manner, however, suggested that he had. He was explaining something to Nedra about a tissue culture she had done.

Hurriedly, Lauren set up the day's experiment. Her fingers felt clumsy. More than once, she dropped a slide as she tried to insert it into the clamps which would hold it securely under the lens of the microscope. She was glad when the class was over.

As she was making her way through the rush of students in the hall, Lauren was surprised to see Miss Emerson's nephew Andrew lounging against the wall, a book tucked casually under his arm. He didn't appear to notice her.

He was a student, after all, she thought as she walked to the union cafeteria. That explained everything. But as she stood in line, waiting for the people in front of her to make their selections, it occurred to her that she had never noticed Andrew in the hall of the Life Science Building before. Of course, that didn't mean anything. She passed hundreds of students each time she went on campus. Hundreds of faces she probably wouldn't recognize if she saw them right now.

She selected a veal cutlet, a small salad, and coffee, then looked around the crowded cafeteria for an empty table, part of her mind still thinking that in the past five days she had run into Andrew in three different places—the Nite Owl, her apartment building, and now the Life Science Building. Coincidence?

"Hey, look who's here!"

She turned to see Kelso and Foxy Freddy at a table for four.

"Why don't you join us?" Freddy offered.

"Thanks," Lauren said gratefully.

"I hear you're coming to our party Saturday night." Kelso got up and helped her with her chair.

"Yes, I am." Lauren removed the dishes from her tray. "I'm looking forward to it. Will Angie and Bets be there?"

Kelso glowered.

"Bets will be," Freddy said, "but Angie and Kelso are on the outs right now."

She flushed. "Oh, I'm sorry."

"It's okay," Kelso said indifferently. "Angie and I were no permanent act, anyway."

Lauren didn't quite know what to say to that, so she changed the subject. "Freddy, there's something I wanted to ask you about Professor Bell."

He made a face. "What about him?"

"When we were talking about him last Saturday night, didn't you say that his wife had left him?"

"Yeah. So what?"

"This morning someone told me that they were divorced. Is that true?"

Freddy frowned. "Maybe there was a divorce. I'm not sure. But I do know that there were all kinds of rumors going around when they broke up. The word was that the university was trying to hush up some kind of scandal."

"Do you know what it was about?"

Kelso broke in. "Wasn't it just because he was running around with students?"

Freddy shook his head. "He's not the only prof who dates students. I can't see the university firing him because of that. No, it was pretty serious."

"Perversion?" Kelso suggested with a leer.

Freddy grimaced. "Shows where *your* mind is!"

"How about wife beating?" Lauren asked innocently.

Freddy looked at her. "Yes, that's it. Only it wasn't a run-of-the-mill case. Seems to me that he tried to kill her."

"Oh, come on," Kelso said impatiently. "They couldn't hush up an attempted homicide."

Freddy had his mouth full of chocolate cake. "That goes to show how little you know!" he mumbled, wiping the crumbs from his mouth with his napkin. "Frankly, the more I think about it, the more I'm inclined to agree with Angie. Remember, she said that Bell would make a good killer."

"Why do you say that?" Lauren asked.

Freddy put down his fork and said slowly, "Well, obviously he had a love-hate relationship with his wife. Very often that situation arises when the man has not had a good relationship with his mother. You see, most men choose to marry women who remind them in some way—good or bad—of their mothers.''

"What about women?'' Lauren asked. "Do they tend to seek men who remind them of their fathers?''

"Of course.''

"What if a girl never knew her father?''

Freddy rubbed his nose. "Interestingly enough, a child who loses a parent tends to idealize that parent and resent the remaining one, even though the remaining parent is the one who cares and provides for the child.''

"Then the girl who's lost her father——''

"Is likely to spend her life searching for the ideal man,'' Freddy finished. "And of course she never finds him.''

Lauren felt suddenly depressed.

"I think that's all a bunch of baloney,'' Kelso declared. "I mean, to get back to the original subject, you're saying that a guy kills women because he didn't get along with his mother? Well, so what? Lots of people don't get along with their mothers! I fight with mine all the time.''

"But this fellow——'' Freddy shook his head, trying to find the word he wanted.

"Arrested emotional development?'' Lauren offered.

"Exactly!''

"Nuts!'' Kelso said derisively. "That's just a fancy phrase for having hang-ups, and everybody has hang-ups.''

Lauren smiled. "Kelso has a point. Does anybody have a really happy home life?''

Kelso smiled at her. "That's just what I'm trying to say! I mean, half the kids I know come from single-parent homes, and they—the kids—get along just fine.'' He turned to Lauren. "Look at me! My folks split up ten years ago. We had money problems, medical problems, all kinds of problems. And have you ever met anybody more normal than I am?''

Freddy screwed up his face. "Quit trying to make a joke of it, Kelso! Most people learn to work out their problems and live with them. But then some people——''

Lauren drained the last of her coffee and jumped up.

"I'm sorry I have to walk out on this fascinating discussion, but I have to be at work at one."

Before she left the dining room, she turned to wave. Kelso was expounding some theory of his while Freddy wore an expression of helplessness.

When she reached Kincaid, Lauren went directly to the cold room. She felt a vague sense of uneasiness as she entered. Before turning off the power packs to stop the electrophoretic process, she noted the voltage of each one. They all checked out.

She looked at her watch. The run had been exactly seventeen hours. Beautiful! This afternoon she would stain the gels with a specially prepared dye and read and record her results.

She hurried down the hall to 207. When she reached the open door, she was surprised to see Dr. Herbert talking with two unfamiliar men.

Broken glass was scattered all over the lab, and the walls and floor were stained with blood.

CHAPTER TWENTY

Lauren stared in disbelief at the destruction all around her. Shards of broken flasks and beakers were strewn over the workbenches and on the floor. Test tubes—some full of blood—had been hurled at the walls. One of the overhead light fixtures was smashed.

Dr. Herbert turned to her. "Oh, Miss Walker, I'm glad you're here. But please don't touch anything. These two gentlemen are from the police. They haven't finished taking fingerprints yet." He turned to the detectives. "This is Lauren Walker, one of my technicians."

The two men acknowledged her presence with barely visible nods. The taller one, a thin man with a large hooked nose, asked, "When were you here last?"

"Yesterday evening. I left shortly after eight."

"Everything in order then?"

"Yes, of course."

"Anyone else around when you left?"

"There are always people in various parts of the building. I didn't notice anyone who shouldn't have been here," Lauren answered.

Dr. Herbert sighed with impatience. "This is really a waste of time! It's obvious who did this and why."

Lauren stared at him. "Paul?"

"Who else?" He turned to the detectives. "You won't find any stranger's fingerprints here, I'm sure. And since Paul's would naturally be all over the lab, I don't see how we can prove a thing."

Lauren remembered the look of hatred that she'd seen in Paul's face yesterday. She had a vision of him smashing glassware, opening the refrigerator and yanking out the

145

racks of blood samples, hurling them around the room, splashing blood everywhere. A broken bottle lay on the floor. Gray-green streaks on the wall above testified to the strength of the acid that the bottle had once contained. Paul must have gone completely out of his mind.

"You'll pay for this!" he'd said.

With a sudden sinking feeling in the pit of her stomach, Lauren hurried back into the cold room. As soon as she opened the door, she knew what she had only sensed before. It was too warm. A glance at the thermostat told her that someone had set the temperature up. Just five degrees centigrade. Just enough to make the results of all her tests questionable. All that work—all that painstaking checking and double-checking—was useless. She felt like crying.

She checked the temperature recorder. The needle had begun a steady ascent around three o'clock in the morning. The steep angle of the needle's rise showed that Paul had not only turned up the thermostat, he had deliberately held the door of the cold room open for a while.

Somehow the mental picture of Paul doing that seemed more frightening than the vision of him smashing glassware and throwing blood around the lab. This was an act of vengeance. And it was directed against *her*.

She returned to 207 and reported the ruined tests to Dr. Herbert, who shook his head in disbelief.

The shorter of the two detectives was taking photographs. When he was done, the insurance examiner arrived.

"The loss is not so great in dollars," Dr. Herbert told him, "but in work! It will take us at least two weeks to duplicate what he has ruined."

For the rest of the day Lauren and Dr. Herbert sifted through the wreckage, pulling labels off broken test tubes in order to determine which blood samples must be reordered, estimating the kinds and amounts of glassware that must be replaced, and generally cleaning up.

It was after nine by the time Lauren left Kincaid. She stopped at a convenience store and picked up some cold cuts, milk and bread. *I'll have a sandwich and go straight to bed,* she promised herself, *I need a good night's sleep.*

But when she stepped into her apartment, she felt her muscles tighten. Something was wrong. She set the groceries on the table and cautiously looked around the apartment. Everything appeared to be as she had left it that morning. The bottles and glasses along the windowsills were undisturbed. The towel she'd flung over the top of the shower curtain rod was still there.

It's just your nerves, she told herself, trying to relax.

She made herself a sandwich but found that she could eat only half of it. She wrapped the remainder in waxed paper and put it in the refrigerator.

What I need is for Terry to call, she thought as she forced herself to finish a glass of milk. It was impossible to talk with him and not feel cheered up. And Kobelski. What about him? she wondered as she got ready for bed. Was he ever going to show up again?

As soon as she closed her eyes, she saw smashed glass and blood all over the lab. *Kobelski really ought to know about that,* she thought. *And about Paul's threatening me, too.*

Maybe Kobelski already knew. He seemed to know everything. But he couldn't know that she was going to meet Professor Bell for dinner tomorrow night, could he? Or about the rumors that Bell was violent?

He still ought to be here. He ought to tell me what to do, how to handle a potentially dangerous situation. She pulled the sheet up under her chin. *He ought to reassure me,* she thought with no small trace of bitterness.

She was tired, but sound sleep wouldn't come. Once she drifted into a dream. Her father had taken her by the hand and was leading her through a dark house. There were large moving shadows everywhere. She was afraid. She called to her father and he turned to her. But he had no face.

"Daddy!"

The sound of her own voice wakened her and she sat up in bed. She was perspiring and yet she felt cold. Why couldn't she see her father's face in her dreams? She seemed to have a clear mental image of him when she was awake. He was a tall, good-looking man with thick dark hair. . . .

She suddenly realized that he looked a lot like Doug. Was that why she had been attracted to Douglas Martin?

Thinking about Doug awakened her completely. She still hadn't decided what she would say to him on Friday. She'd been avoiding the whole problem because she didn't want to have to make a decision. And yet she must. When Doug showed up on Friday, she had to know exactly what to say and how to say it. She had to have her emotions under control. Strange. It was as if she were preparing for a battle instead of a meeting with a man she'd loved—still did love—and nearly married.

At first, when they became engaged, everything had seemed so right. It didn't seem important that Doug's parents weren't entirely pleased, that they thought Lauren didn't come from the right kind of family. She wouldn't fit in with their friends.

It would work out all right, Doug had assured her confidently. Once she was Mrs. Douglas Martin, she would be accepted.

Doug was very close to his parents. As the eldest child and only son—his sister was three years younger—he had had both overgenerosity and overexpectation heaped upon him. Looking back now, Lauren marveled that he had never buckled beneath those expectations and defied his parents.

But he *had*, she suddenly realized. He'd become engaged to her, a working girl from the lower middle class. She had never before appreciated what an enormous step that must have been for him. Nor had she completely realized what a blow it must have been to him when she broke the engagement. His parents probably never actually said, ''We told you so!'' but the message must have been there, and how Doug must have hated it! She wondered whether he'd gotten some satisfaction from the breakup of his marriage. Had that, in a way, been a punishment for his parents?

She shook the idea from her mind. What had happened was done with, and Doug's motives were known only to him. Her problem was to decide what was going to happen now. Could she be happy married to Douglas Martin? What kind of a marriage did she want? *For better or for worse,* she thought. *I want the real thing!*

And Doug—what did he expect? Only the better part, clearly. When things had taken a turn for the worse, he gave Nancy only a few months. If she—Lauren—married him and didn't live up to his expectations, then what? He'd probably walk out on her, too. The way Daddy had walked out on Ma.

Her chest grew suddenly tight. The comparison was painful. For a moment she had a terrifying thought. Perhaps she was genetically programmed to be just like her mother. Perhaps, in spite of herself, she would end up marrying a man who didn't really love her.

No! She buried her face into her pillow. She'd never do that! She'd never even be foolish enough to take that chance! Which meant, she realized, that she *must* say no to Doug again.

That decision made, she felt strangely calm. Somewhere deep inside, she had known all along what she was going to do.

CHAPTER TWENTY-ONE

She was wide awake again. Maybe some warm milk and soft music would help. She put a pan of milk on the stove and removed the fern from the dust cover of the record player and set it on the bookcase. The plant looked better already, she thought distractedly as she put a record on the turntable. Miss Emerson certainly knew her stuff.

It was midnight. She still felt tense. The warm milk and the music had not brought sleep any closer. *Blast Kobelski!* she thought, pulling her housecoat more tightly around her. *It's all his fault. I'm worried about so many things at once. I've got to talk to him!*

But where was he? She hadn't seen him since Sunday. Ages ago. He hadn't been kidding when he said he'd fade into the background. Not once had she been aware of his presence outside of the times he'd come to her apartment. He was good at his business. Too good?

Lauren suddenly realized that she had no way of being certain that Kobelski was around at all. What if something had happened to him? A car accident? A heart attack? What if she were in danger and she screamed, but he didn't come?

She wished the thought had never occurred to her. Up to now, she'd placed her confidence in Kobelski's nearness. Now that she doubted his presence, the walls seemed to be crumbling around her. *Was he there?* There was only one way to find out. She took a deep breath and screamed.

Almost instantly, there was a knock at the door. Relieved, Lauren ran to the door and threw it open. But only Miss Emerson stood in the foyer. She was wrapped in her lavender robe with the high neck of an old-fashioned lace-trimmed nightgown covering her throat. "Are you all right, dearie? I heard a scream."

Lauren flushed with embarrassment. "Quite all right," she assured the little woman. "I—I opened the broom closet and a mouse ran out. I'm terrified of mice."

Miss Emerson looked right through her. Her mouth was smiling but her eyes were not. "Of course, dearie. Well, as long as everything's all right, I'll leave you."

After she'd gone, Lauren leaned against the door and covered her face with her hands. *So that's how Kobelski's going to protect me!* she thought. *I scream and all that happens is that a little old lady comes to my door! A lot of good Miss Emerson could have done if someone had been strangling me!*

Where on earth *was* Kobelski?

And what was she going to do now? Maybe just pack a suitcase and clear out. But where could she go? If only——

There was a soft rap on the door.

"Who is it?"

"Kobelski. Let me in."

She hurried to open the door. "You little idiot," he growled as he entered. "Don't you know better than to cry wolf?"

"Don't call me names!" Lauren retorted angrily. "And where were *you?* Why didn't you come right away?"

He grabbed her wrist. "Calm down. There were people outside, and I didn't want to take the risk of being seen."

"You didn't want to take a risk! What about *me?* I could have been killed!" Furious, she wrenched her arm free from his grasp.

"Take it easy," he said mildly. "I'm trying to tell you that I knew you were all right."

She turned on him. "How could you *know*? Just because you didn't see anyone enter my apartment? What if someone had been hiding in the closet since this afternoon? He could have strangled me ten times over before you came!"

Kobelski seemed amused, and he pulled her toward him again. His amusement angered her, and her anger heightened the strain of the day's events. Her emotions were overtaking her, and she knew that she was going to cry no matter how hard she tried not to.

In sheer frustration she pounded Kobelski's chest with her fist. "Damn you! I should have known you'd let me down!"

His attitude changed instantly. He grabbed her shoulders and shook her gently. "I didn't let you down, Lauren. When I promised I would protect you, I meant it! I knew there was no one hiding in here."

She looked at him, aware that tears were rolling down her cheeks. "How could you be sure?"

He drew a deep breath and let it out again, puffing his cheeks in the process. "Because I checked. Before you came home." He grinned. "I looked in the closet. And in the shower and under the bed, too!"

Lauren stared at him. She knew he was telling the truth. That was why she had felt someone had been in the apartment. Nothing she could put her finger on, but *something*—an intangible something—had registered his presence.

Her anger returned and with it a generous measure of fear. "You told me you wouldn't sneak in here again. You promised!"

Kobelski wandered over to the window and carefully moved the shade to one side, making sure that he didn't disturb the line of bottles on the sill. He looked out for a moment, then dropped the shade back into place.

Watching him, Lauren wondered how much she could trust him. "We made a deal and you lied to me!" she said bitterly.

"It wasn't a very big lie." His voice was so low that she could hardly hear him. Oddly, that made her even angrier.

"I'm putting my life in your hands, Kobelski! That makes any lie big!"

He was silent for a moment. "You're right," he admitted. "I apologize. Friends?"

She shook her head. "I don't know. Why did you do it?"

He shrugged. "You said it yourself. Your life's in my hands. I had to make sure the place was safe. I knew you were hung up on privacy, but I figured what you didn't know wouldn't hurt you. I was wrong."

It was the longest speech she had ever heard him make, and he seemed genuinely humble.

"Will you keep your promise now?"

He gave her a pained look. "I can't. Your safety comes first. Don't you see? Maybe Diane and Ellen didn't let this guy in."

"You mean if you can get in and out so easily, maybe he can, too?"

"Right."

"Why can't I just have some good strong locks installed?"

"You're supposed to be bait, remember?" He was impatient now. "You can't live behind a bunch of locks." He paused. "And I don't want all that junk on the windowsills, either."

She considered. "Well, suppose I agree to let you check out the apartment before I come home. Would you promise not to sneak in when I'm here?"

"Deal. Unless I think you're in danger. Then all bets are off."

"Okay," she said slowly. "I guess I can live with that."

Kobelski gave a huge mock sigh of relief. "Now that we've got that settled, why *did* you scream?"

"I had to talk to you. You know, we really need a signal. Something that says I'm not in danger but want to get in touch."

"Good idea." He looked around the room. "This'll do it," he said, walking over to the bookcase and picking up the fern in the red pot. "When you want to talk, put it in the window. I'll be in as soon as the coast is clear."

Lauren nodded. Then she told him about Paul's rampage in the lab. "He completely freaked out. The place was a shambles. And he threatened me, too."

"He bears watching, all right," Kobelski said. "I've

already done some checking. He's a former mental patient, you know."

She looked at him. "No, I *didn't* know. What's wrong with him?"

He shook his head. "So far, all I've learned is that he comes from a quiet, respectable family. No apparent problems there."

Lauren frowned. "I wonder—I tried to pump him about his family yesterday. When I asked him about his mother, he hesitated before answering me. He said that they were very close but I felt he was too insistent. Couldn't his psychiatrist tell you about that?"

Kobelski shook his head again. "Details like that take a while. There's the problem of confidentiality. You have to check such things out in a roundabout way."

"If you're always watching me, when do you have time to do all this checking?"

He grinned. "Trade secret."

"No, seriously."

"Seriously, then. I don't need much time. Just connections." Without asking, he opened the refrigerator, found a can of Coke, opened it and gulped it down. "Last one," he said, wiping his mouth with the back of his hand. "Hope you don't mind."

"I'll put it on my expense account," she said flippantly as she plopped into the easy chair. He was a strange man, she thought. Sometimes, like now when he was grinning at her, he was so very likable. At other times, he made her angrier than anyone she'd ever known.

"By the way," he said. "I thought you'd like to know that you were right about the Kelso fellow's alibi. It's not ironclad after all. The five of them—Richard, his father, two business associates, and a guide—went on a fishing trip from Friday afternoon until Monday night."

Lauren interrupted. "And Dee Dee was killed when?"

"The time wasn't definitely established. She had worked until one o'clock on Sunday morning, when the Nite Owl closed. No one saw her after that until they found her body on Tuesday evening. The medical examiner's estimate was somewhere between one-thirty A.M. and six P.M. on Sunday."

"Then, if Kelso was on that fishing trip until Monday night, why isn't he in the clear?"

"Because there was a twelve-hour period when he wasn't with the others."

"*What?*"

"The men decided to go into town on Saturday night for steaks and entertainment. They ended up getting into an all-night poker game and didn't get back to the cabin until six-thirty in the morning."

"So?"

"So Richard didn't go into town with them. He claimed he had a bad headache and stayed at the cabin."

"He does get bad headaches. Terry told me about them."

"That may be. The fact remains, however, that no one saw him from six o'clock on Saturday evening until six-thirty Sunday morning. And they were only three-and-a-half hours away from here."

"Does that mean that his father did buy him an alibi?"

Kobelski shook his head. "Not necessarily. The men may have said that Kelso was with them the whole time because they considered that he was. After all, the cabin was a hundred and seventy miles away from the scene of the murder."

Lauren frowned. "Terry described Kelso's headaches as incapacitating. Why would he drive all the way down here and back if he were in such pain?"

"The guy we're after isn't necessarily logical when he's in a killing mood," Kobelski said. "Look at it this way: Kelso dated Diane, knew where she worked, where she lived, and what time she'd get home. The way the time works out, he could have been waiting for her when she came home."

"But why?"

"That, doll, is the big question. Anyhow, keep your ears open. Dig up what you can about Kelso."

He stared at her for a moment. "You had an unexpected visitor Monday night, didn't you?"

When she realized that he was talking about Doug, she felt her cheeks grow hot. "That has nothing to do with the murders! He's an old friend."

He looked amused. "I know."

"You checked on him?"

"Of course. Douglas Martin, ex-fiancé. Twenty-four. Lucrative job with his father's company. Presently being divorced by his wife." He stopped and grinned at her. "I don't have to be much of a detective to figure out why he was here."

"Kobelski!" she fumed. "You are outrageous!"

"Take it easy," he said mildly. "It's important that I know who's nibbling at my bait and why. But I'll try to keep your private life intact."

"There's nothing private about my life anymore," she sighed.

"That comes with the territory," he said flatly. "Anything else I need to know?"

She told him about Professor Bell's invitation to dinner. "Nedra Hines says he's violent. He used to beat his wife. Any tips on how to handle him?"

Kobelski looked thoughtful. "You're eating at the union?"

"Yes. The faculty dining room."

"I don't think there's any problem as long as you're in a public place, but I'll be keeping an eye on you anyway. The problems start when he wants to be alone with you."

"Do you think he will?" she asked anxiously.

He smiled. "Bell's not blind, is he?"

She colored. "What should I do if he wants to—to be alone?"

He thought about it for a moment. "Might not be a bad idea to suggest coming here. He lives at the University Club, and I don't think he'd take you there."

Lauren agreed. "No matter how broad-minded they are, the board of regents wouldn't approve of a professor taking a different young woman to his rooms every other day.''

''Right. So he'll probably jump at the chance to come here.''

Lauren made a face at the thought. ''Nedra said something else today—I don't know whether it's important.''

What's that?''

''His ex-wife took him for a ride in the divorce settlement. She got everything. He could easily hate her.''

''Probably does,'' Kobelski agreed. ''So?''

''So she's a blonde. I might remind him of her.''

His eyebrows went up. ''Good!''

''Is it? That's another thing that bothers me.''

''What is?''

''I remind everybody of someone else! I feel unreal. As if Lauren Walker doesn't exist anymore.''

''Take it easy. We're creating an illusion, remember? Don't get caught up in it.''

''It's not easy to be an illusion,'' she grumbled.

He squatted beside her chair so that he could look directly into her eyes. The lines of his face softened. ''To a certain extent, we're all illusions,'' he said gently. ''What you see when you look at me is only your perception of me. Perhaps nothing could be further from the truth.''

''No two people see things in the same light, is that it?''

''I guess so.''

She sighed. ''You're right, of course. I think what's really bothering me is that I'm imagining what other people are thinking of me. Like today—Bell made sure the whole class knew that we were having dinner together tomorrow.''

''Nice guy, isn't he?'' Kobelski said sarcastically.

''The strange thing is that, as a teacher, he is nice. He's a marvelous teacher. I really admire him. But outside the classroom, I don't like him or the idea of being alone with him.''

''Scared?''

She nodded.

He stood up, extended a hand and pulled her from her chair. ''You won't exactly be alone,'' he said softly. ''Trust me?''

Lauren hesitated only a fraction of a second before nodding.

He put his hand beneath her chin and raised her face to his. "Don't worry," he whispered. His lips were warm and tender. He brushed them against her mouth, then pressed hard. His strong arms encircled her and for the first time in—how long?—Lauren felt *safe*.

It was over in a moment. Kobelski had a hard time meeting her eyes. "See you tomorrow," he said abruptly and turned to leave.

"Kobelski?"

"Yeah?"

"Are you married?"

He looked at her over his shoulder. "No."

"Ever been?"

"Yes."

He obviously wasn't going to say any more, and Lauren couldn't think of a suitable remark. The silence became embarrassing.

Finally, he asked, "What's on your mind?"

"I was thinking," she said. "If you said that I reminded you of her, I'd scream."

He laughed out loud and shook his head. "You don't look anything like her." He paused for a moment, then added, "You're beautiful too. But definitely different."

Lauren stared at the door after he'd gone. She still felt Kobelski's lips burning against hers. And he had called her beautiful. But he had lied to her as well, she reminded herself.

CHAPTER TWENTY-TWO

It seemed to Lauren that she had hardly fallen asleep when the phone on the nightstand rang. Half-awake, she groped for the receiver in the dark.

"Laurie? Laurie, I need you." The words were slurred together. Her heart sank as she recognized her mother's voice. She flicked on the bedside lamp. The clock said two-thirty.

"What's the matter, Ma?"

Deep racking sobs came over the line. "Oh, Laurie, my baby! I need you!" More sobs. A long string of unintelligible words.

Lauren wondered whether her mother had been drinking. She seldom did when Aunt Lil was around. Unless something was terribly wrong. "Ma, I can't understand you! What's happened?"

"Please come here and stay with me." More sobs.

"Ma, put Aunt Lil on the line."

"We called earlier. You weren't home," her aunt said brusquely a moment later. "I told her to wait until morning, but her sleeping pill wore off a little while ago. I couldn't settle her down. She said she had to call you now."

Lauren could almost see Aunt Lil. Her lips set in a hard, tight line, her steel-gray hair severely pulled back into a twist. Her pinched face, her angry eyes.

"Aunt Lil, what's going on?"

"Your father's dead. The good-for-nothing scum was killed in a bar. A knifing, they said."

Lauren closed her eyes. She felt a tightness in her chest which made her gasp for breath. "When—when did it happen?"

"Three weeks ago. On the waterfront in San Francisco. But we just found out about it today—I mean yesterday."

Three weeks ago. A sharp pain shot through Lauren's body. It was as if she'd been split into two people. One Lauren wanted to cry, "Oh, Daddy! How could you leave me again?" The other Lauren felt angry. *Don't be stupid,* she told herself. *Why should you cry over a man you haven't seen in nineteen years? A man who didn't care enough to remember even one of those nineteen birthdays?*

She realized that she was clutching the receiver so tightly that her fingers ached. She switched hands and drew a deep breath. Practical matters first. "Aunt Lil, Ma sounds pretty bad."

"She is. I'm afraid she might—I think you ought to be here."

Lauren hesitated. She remembered her last weeks at home. "I don't know if I can make it," she said slowly. "Besides, what she really needs is to be hospitalized."

"Hospitalized!" Aunt Lil's voice dripped with sarcasm. "Hospitals cost money. Your ma has no insurance and she's too young for Medicare. Besides, she's still paying the bills from last time!"

"But Aunt Lil——"

"*I* haven't got that kind of money!"

"*I'll* pay for it!" Lauren heard herself shouting.

How on earth was she going to do it? Never mind. She'd manage somehow. The important thing was to get Ma in a hospital as soon as possible. She must be kept under constant watch for a while.

". . . at least a hundred-and-fifty dollars a day," Aunt Lil was saying.

"I'll wire you the money," Lauren said quickly. "Just get her in first thing in the morning. And don't leave her alone, even for a short time."

"Where are you going to get that kind of money?" Aunt Lil did not try to hide the suspicion from her voice.

"I'll get it!" Lauren hung up.

She sat on the bed, her hand still resting on the receiver. Tears were streaming down her cheeks. It was crazy. She

had never really known the man who had been her father.
All she'd ever had was a few fuzzy memories. Then why
did she feel that she'd lost everything now? Why did she
feel so alone?

She wished she hadn't hung up so quickly. She should
have tried to talk to Ma some more. To calm her down. She
should have asked about the funeral. Or had there already
been one? Had they buried him in San Francisco? They?
Who? Had her father acquired a new family somewhere?

Not that she could afford a trip out west, anyhow. And if
she were going anywhere at all, she ought to go to Florida
and stay with Ma. And yet, she wished she could see her
father, if only in death. She flopped over the bed, buried her
face in her pillow and cried.

Funny. It made perfect sense to cry. For so many years,
she'd hated her mother's self-pity and felt only contempt for
a display of tears. But she understood it now. Ma was
suffering more than the loss of a person. And more than the
loss of someone's love. It was the death of a dream. All
these years, she must have nursed some faint hope of his
return.

Lauren, too, had always had a dream. One day she'd
meet her father again. He'd put his arms around her. He'd
smell of pipe tobacco and bittersweet-scented after-shave.
And she'd be safe. The way she felt in Kobelski's arms
tonight.

Lauren tried again to remember her father. A knifing on
the waterfront? Was that what he'd been like? Had she—as
Freddy had suggested—only fantasized the gentle, sensitive
man who'd tossed her into the air when she was a little
child?

It occurred to her that instead of Doug's resembling her
father, she might have used the traits that she found most
attractive in Doug to construct a memory of her father. How
could she be sure what her father had looked like? Ma hadn't
kept any pictures—none that Lauren had seen. So Lauren
had only her memories. And how much could a three-year-
old truly remember?

Of course, a man could change a lot in nineteen years.

But that much? And if he had always been a—a good-for-nothing, as Aunt Lil had called him, what did that make her?

She suddenly realized that she had never considered herself her mother's child. Only her father's. It always disturbed her to see resemblances between herself and Ma, and she strove to be as different a person as possible. All of her good points she'd attributed to her father. Once, when a high school teacher had commented that Lauren had an unusually perceptive mind, she'd blurted, "My father did, too." The words had popped out of nowhere, but she'd believed them. And so her father's intelligence became another of her "remembrances."

Had it all been an illusion? As a child, she had often looked into the mirror and searched for traces of her father in her face. Now she looked across the room and stared into the glass above her bureau. But of course she didn't even look like Lauren Walker anymore.

What was happening to her? The tears started coming again, and she let them flow freely.

CHAPTER TWENTY-THREE

Lauren awoke with the feeling of having had a bad dream. Then she remembered the telephone call. Had it actually happened? Had she really promised Aunt Lil that she would wire enough money to keep Ma in the hospital?

She did a little mental arithmetic. She had nearly two hundred and fifty dollars in her savings account—that was supposed to go toward next semester's tuition. Add to that the two hundred Kobelski had given her on Sunday . . . Strictly speaking, that money wasn't hers to do with as she pleased, but where else could she raise cash? The student credit union? Not when she was only a part-time student. The bank? She had no collateral. Her car was too old to even be considered.

She could keep her mother in the hospital for three days at best. That wasn't enough. Last time—could it have been only two months ago?—the doctor had said a minimum of two weeks. But that had been an actual suicide attempt. Did it make a difference? Two weeks in the hospital would cost over two thousand dollars! There was no way out. She would have to go to Florida and stay with Ma for a couple of weeks.

Lauren got up and dressed. Her eyes were still swollen from crying. It was going to take a real makeup job to disguise that, she thought ruefully.

She pulled her suitcase out from under the bed and started packing. It was still too early to call Dr. Herbert. She'd have to leave a message for Professor Bell, too. Who else? Mrs. Harper. The rent was paid for the next three weeks, so that wasn't an immediate problem, although finding next month's rent might be.

Kobelski. She might as well tell him right now. She put the fern in the living room window and continued packing. She dug into the cardboard box at the back of the closet to get some summer things. She needn't take much. Just a few things which she could rinse out easily. With a pang, she realized that she mustn't give Ma the impression that she was there to stay.

A knock on the door interrupted her thoughts.

"What's——" Kobelski stopped when he saw her. "You look terrible." He frowned. "What's wrong?"

"My father's dead," she said tersely. "I've got to go away for a while."

He stared at her for a moment. "I'm sorry about your father," he said slowly. "Do you mean you're going to the funeral?"

She shook her head. "To Florida. My mother's pretty broken up about it. In her condition—well, you know about that. She has to be watched."

Kobelski touched her cheek with his fingertips. "Looks like she's not the only one who's been having a rough time."

Lauren turned away. "It's stupid to cry about it," she said bitterly. "It's no big tragedy. I didn't even know the man."

"Maybe that's the tragedy," he murmured. He was silent for a moment. Then he said, "You can't go."

She looked at him angrily. "Didn't you hear me? She can't be left alone! And Aunt Lil can't watch her twenty-four hours a day!"

"There are hospitals."

"We haven't got the money for a hospital, Kobelski!"

"I'll take care of it," he said quietly. "A good hospital and round-the-clock nursing care."

"That takes money."

"My expense account's not limited."

"You can't use Rickover's money! This hasn't got anything to do with your job!"

He clamped his lips together for a moment. Then he said

slowly, "Lauren, this guy is going to kill again—and soon. I know it! If you're not here to bait him, he may just go after someone else."

She hadn't considered that possibility. She thought of Ellen and Dee Dee. The smiling faces in Kobelski's photos. She couldn't be responsible for another girl's death. Finally she said, "Okay, I'll stay. You get some money to my aunt, and I'll straighten things out with Mr. Rickover later. Somehow."

"Lauren, you help me nab the guy who killed Ellen and you won't owe Tom Rickover anything."

"You'll need my aunt's name and address."

He shook his head. "I've already got it. I'll wire the money. She'll have it this afternoon."

A moment later, he was gone. To stand in a shadow, waiting. Watching. What a lonely occupation. It occurred to her that Kobelski was a lonely man. A sad, lonely man.

CHAPTER TWENTY-FOUR

Lauren arrived at work an hour late and spent the rest of the morning trying to reorganize the lab. She had to borrow glassware from other laboratories in the Institute. There were insurance forms to fill out and letters to write, reordering the blood samples from a half-dozen hospitals.

Although the work wasn't difficult, she found it hard to keep her mind on what she was doing. She'd had very little sleep last night, and she felt emotionally drained, worried about Ma and nervous about her dinner that evening with Professor Bell.

And in a little more than twenty-four hours, Doug would be back, expecting her answer. And she didn't know how she was going to tell him that she still couldn't marry him. There was no way she could handle the situation without hurting him. She dreaded having to face him. For a moment she considered staying away from the apartment and just leaving him a note taped to the door.

Coward! she said to herself as she sealed an envelope. *There's only one way to do it, and that's face to face.* The truth didn't make her feel any better.

At noon, Dr. Herbert came in. "Paul is missing," he announced. "The police say his landlady hasn't seen him since Tuesday evening. His things are still in his apartment."

Lauren looked at him. "What do the police think has happened to him?"

"That he's either run away or is hiding. I think he's out of his mind."

Lauren drew a deep breath. Now was as good a time as

any to try to explain to him why Paul had been so upset. She told him how Paul had been questioned about Ellen's murder. "He is awfully unsure of himself—he's been treated for mental illness in the past," she finished.

Dr. Herbert looked at her sharply. "How do you know that?"

Lauren bit her lip. "He—told me." She couldn't tell the professor about Kobelski. "And then, when I had my hair cut, he seemed to think that I looked a lot like El—like the dead girl. He got the idea that there was some kind of a conspiracy against him."

Dr. Herbert shook his head. "Well, no matter what he thinks, it's obvious that he's not able to do useful work."

"But he needs *help!*"

Dr. Herbert peered at her over the top of his rimless glasses. "My dear, what do you expect me to do?"

Lauren flushed. "I don't know," she admitted. "There must be something."

"Well, we'll see. When the police find him, perhaps I can arrange for the charges to be lessened if he seeks treatment."

He didn't sound enthusiastic. Lauren knew that Dr. Herbert felt more resentment toward Paul's destruction of the lab than he would have felt if someone had vandalized his home. The lab was really where he lived.

Terry called her in the afternoon. "I hope it's not against the rules for me to call you at work," he said. "I just wondered how your exam went yesterday. And I thought you might like to study tonight with me—and maybe have a couple of beers afterward."

"Oh!" Disappointment sounded in Lauren's voice as she thought of her dinner engagement with Professor Bell. "I'd love to, Terry, but I'm afraid I can't. There's—something I have to take care of this evening. I don't know how long it'll take."

She felt deceitful and wished she could explain to him exactly why she couldn't see him. But after their talk last

Saturday night about Warren Bell, she just couldn't bring herself to say that she was having dinner with him to talk about her classwork. Nor could she explain that she was seeing him on Kobelski's orders.

"Hey, that's all right," Terry said easily. "I'll miss you, but I'll just look forward that much more to seeing you on Saturday."

"Thanks," Lauren said gratefully. She was looking forward to Saturday, too. It seemed to her that the good-natured craziness of Terry and his friends had been the only bit of sanity she'd encountered in the past week.

"Is everything all right?" he asked. "You sound—I don't know—upset."

Lauren almost told him about her father before she remembered that she had already told Terry that her father had died nineteen years ago. Why on earth had she lied to him? She was tempted to tell him the truth. Terry would be sympathetic; he'd say the right thing and make her feel better. But she couldn't admit that she'd lied to him. Probably because she couldn't explain it even to herself. "I've had a lot of problems at work," she said finally. That was true enough.

"I'm sorry," Terry responded sincerely. "Wish I could help."

"You already have." Lauren smiled to herself. *That* was certainly true.

The faculty dining room was on the third floor of the student union. In contrast to the glass and stainless steel of the cafeteria on the first floor, the faculty dining room had plush carpeting and drapes, and soft indirect lighting accented by wall sconces resembling candelabra. An exhibit of the works by the university's artist-in-residence hung on one wall. Soft violin music was being played in the background.

Lauren stood in the doorway and looked around for Warren Bell.

He was already seated at a table. He wore a denim suit

that made him look ten years younger. When he saw her, he smiled. He got up and came over to her. "Ah, there you are! I was lucky enough to get a table by the window. We can look out on the lake." He helped her with her chair. "I'm so glad that we're having this evening together," he said. "I meant what I said the other day—that I was impressed with your work. You have a fine mind, Lauren. We need young women like you in the sciences."

"Thank you," she said, uncomfortable at the unexpected praise.

After the waitress had taken their orders, he went on, "Tell me about your plans for the future. With your talents, you ought to be a full-time student. And you should consider getting a doctorate."

Lauren explained her financial difficulties. "Having done my undergraduate work at a small college didn't help matters any," she added.

"Perhaps not. There are a lot of prejudices in the university community. However, a personal recommendation can sometimes overcome such obstacles." He paused eloquently. "I have a good friend in the department who will have a research assistantship available next semester."

Lauren stared at him. A research assistantship would enable her to go to school full-time. Since Bell didn't know about her arrangement with Kobelski, it was a very attractive offer for him to make. Unless there were strings attached. "That would be very nice," she said, trying to put more enthusiasm into her voice than she felt.

While the waitress was serving their salad, Lauren tried to steer the conversation in a different direction. "How long have you been here at the university?"

Bell seemed pleased at the chance to talk about himself. "Fourteen years. I came here right out of graduate school."

"You must have had a lot of different students in all that time."

"Oh, yes. I teach freshman biology during the spring session, you know. In that class alone, there are a couple hundred students."

"I don't suppose you remember any one student for very long, then."

"Certain ones I remember quite well," he said in a slightly offended tone.

"Do you remember Ellen Rickover?"

He frowned. "Rickover? Rickover. Small dark girl with glasses?"

Lauren watched him closely but could not tell whether he was acting. "Wrong girl, I'm afraid. Ellen was in your freshman biology class last year."

"Well, that explains it," he said easily. "I don't really get to know anyone in a class that size. Is there some reason why I should remember her?"

"She was murdered a few weeks ago."

"Oh, *that* girl! I remember reading about it in the papers. I didn't even know she was in my class."

His voice sounded natural enough, Lauren thought.

He looked at her with curiosity. "Was she a friend of yours?"

Lauren shook her head. "No. Just a friend of a friend, actually." Was it her imagination, or did he seem to relax a bit at her words?

"I'm very sorry about her. But murder isn't a pleasant subject at dinnertime," he said as the waitress returned with the main course. "Let's talk about you. I like to know about my students."

She told him vaguely about herself, omitting all the unpleasant details.

"Then you're a native midwesterner," Bell said. "That's nice. I mean, you get to visit your family fairly often."

Lauren explained that she had no family except her mother and aunt and that both of them lived in Florida.

A new spark of interest showed in his face. "So you have no one in this part of the country?"

Lauren shook her head.

"Well, I do hope you'll consider me a friend," he said with a warm smile.

Later, while he was instructing the waitress about coffee

and dessert, Lauren got a chance to study him closely. He was good-looking, without a doubt. The soft lighting of the room flattered his craggy features and enhanced the illusion of youth. He was deeply tanned. Probably from a sunlamp, or he wouldn't be so dark at this time of year. It did look nice, though. Especially with his blond hair. He had a good barber—stylist, rather—for his hair was cut painstakingly. As she looked at it, she was startled to see that the roots were dark.

He bleaches his hair! She could hardly keep from smiling.

"Something amuses you," he said. "What is it?"

Lauren colored. "I was admiring your haircut," she stammered. "It's very nice."

"Why, thank you." His face showed his pleasure.

She bent her head as she rearranged her napkin on her lap. She felt oddly guilty about the white lie. Of course, it had been the only polite thing to say, but it seemed to her that more and more she was lying, speaking half-truths, hiding her feelings and, perhaps, losing touch with what was real and what wasn't.

Maybe it was a necessary part of creating the illusion that Kobelski wanted. Still, it gave her the uneasy feeling that she was changing, that the change was beyond her control, and that when it was all over she would never be the same.

"Shall we?" Warren Bell stood up and helped her with her chair. He put his hand beneath her elbow as she rose.

"Now, what do you say to a little liquid refreshment?" he asked as they walked to the elevator.

Lauren felt her temper rising. He was as good as admitting that it had been a charade, that the evening had nothing to do with her work. If it weren't for Kobelski's orders, she'd have told Bell off right then and there. Blast Kobelski!

"If you like," she said lightly.

Lauren's heart sank when she realized that they were heading for the Nite Owl. She could only hope that no one she knew would be there tonight. After all, she consoled herself, she didn't know many students. And it was Thursday. The bar wasn't so likely to be full as on a weekend.

Bell insisted on putting his arm around her shoulders as they entered the bar. There was a good-sized crowd in spite of its being a week night, and the general mood seemed to be one of amiable mischief. We know we should be studying, they all seemed to be saying, but we'd much rather have a good time tonight. We'll get by somehow.

Lauren was relieved that she saw no familiar faces. And the only available table was a small one at the back of the room. *So much the better,* she thought.

A stuffed owl stared at them from a shelf on the wall. Bell moved his chair around next to hers so that they could sit side-by-side. "Much cozier this way." He smiled at her. Some of Lauren's misgivings must have been apparent in her face, for he added, "I'm not such a bad fellow, really. Oh, I know the stories that go around the campus. They're greatly exaggerated, believe me!"

After one glass of beer, Lauren switched to ginger ale. Bell, however, was drinking more than his share. He was happily engrossed in telling her all about himself in great detail and an embarrassingly loud voice. He was Phi Beta Kappa. Graduated *magna cum laude.* Had been on the debating team in college and earned a letter in track. He'd edged out over a hundred candidates for a postdoctoral fellowship. He'd written books, published papers. He, he, he. There was no mention of a wife or family or even a friend. Lauren stifled a yawn. Maybe he didn't have any.

Time passed very slowly. Once or twice when she discreetly glanced at her watch, she was sure it had stopped. As Bell poured himself another glass of beer, she glanced around. There at the bar, where he again had a good view of her in the mirror, was Miss Emerson's nephew, Andrew. He wore the same dark windbreaker with the collar turned up and a sailor cap with the brim turned down. He had to be watching her. He'd been here last Saturday, outside her classroom on Wednesday, at her apartment building on Monday, and here he was again. Four times in the last few days. Hardly a coincidence. She must remember to tell Kobelski about him.

Bell was telling her how he had won academic honors for

his research, when the noise level in the bar escalated abruptly. A new group of students had entered. They were laughing and joking, and several voices greeted them enthusiastically. Lauren looked up to see Terry and some of his friends, including Kelso and Pudge. Terry hadn't yet seen her. He was playfully punching a fellow student who sat at the bar. The two of them were laughing. Panicky, Lauren looked around. Perhaps he wouldn't stay long. If she ducked into the ladies' room . . .

Then Terry turned and saw her. His gaze traveled over to Professor Bell, then back to Lauren. The color and good humor drained out of his face. His eyes were filled with pain.

He's an innocent, Lauren thought with a little shock. *He really believes in angels and fairy princesses.* With a rush of shame, she realized that he had put her on a pedestal. And now it seemed to him that she had come crashing down. Worse yet, it had happened in front of his friends. He turned away from her and sat down next to Pudge. He was going to ignore her. In a way, that was more painful than a confrontation.

"Excuse me for a minute," she said to Bell. "I want to talk to a friend."

She got up and walked over to Terry's table and tapped him on the shoulder. Pudge studiously examined the ceiling. Kelso appeared to be inspecting a fingernail, but Lauren realized that he was watching her out of the corner of his eye.

"Hello, Terry."

He didn't look up.

"May I talk to you?"

He considered for a moment, then slowly got up without a glance at her and walked toward the door.

She went after him. "Terry, wait!"

He turned on her, and there was such a wounded look in his eyes that she felt shot through with pain.

Oh, God! I've really hurt him! "I know this looks pretty bad," she said slowly, "But it isn't what it seems. I can't explain right now——"

"You don't owe me any explanations," he said coldly. "I don't own you. And you did tell me you were busy tonight."

"But——"

"It's a rough world," he cut in. "You have to decide what you want out of life and go after it any way you can. So you need a good grade." He shrugged.

"That's not true!"

"You don't have to lie to me, either."

"I'm not lying."

"You little bitch!" He spoke the words so quietly that for a moment Lauren couldn't believe she'd heard them. Then he turned and walked out the door.

She stared after him, stunned, feeling as though her face had been slapped. He had no right to talk to her like that! She hadn't done anything wrong! He might at least have reserved judgment until he'd heard her side of it.

Professor Bell came up behind her and took her arm. "Shall we leave?" he asked.

Kelso and Pudge were watching her. So was Andrew. So were a lot of other people who knew Warren Bell's reputation. She felt like crying.

Damn Kobelski! This was all his fault!

But it wasn't, of course. He hadn't forced her into anything. She had volunteered. Because of the money. *You have to decide what you want out of life and go after it any way you can.* That was what she had done, wasn't it?

No, it wasn't, she argued with herself. She hadn't done anything wrong. Then why did she feel so terrible? She felt as though a hundred pairs of eyes were on her as they left the Nite Owl.

CHAPTER TWENTY-FIVE

The night air felt cool to her burning face. The music from the jukebox in the Nite Owl faded as they walked down the street.

"Is your car this way?" Bell asked matter-of-factly.

"Yes. About two blocks down," she said as they crossed the street.

"I'll drive you home. I can take a cab back." He added the last sentence quickly, as if he expected her to object. He seemed relieved when she didn't.

At least, Lauren thought, this part was going according to the plan. She would casually invite Bell in when they got to the apartment. She wondered where Kobelski was. She looked around at the shadowy doorways and alleys, at the parked cars. He could be anywhere.

When they reached her car, she rummaged in her purse for her keys, and Bell held out his hand for them. He opened the passenger door for her and, as he circled behind the car to the driver's side, Lauren checked to make certain that the toggle switch was off.

Bell slid behind the wheel. "Don't tell me you're going to sit way over there," he chided her.

Obediently, Lauren moved closer to him. He put his arm around her shoulder and pulled her to his side.

"That's better." He smiled at her as he pulled the car away from the curb. She could smell the beer on his breath. And something else that she hadn't been conscious of before. The scent of bittersweet after-shave. Was it possible, she wondered as they turned a corner, that people who shared certain tastes were somehow alike? Could her father have been someone like Warren Bell? Suddenly overaware of the scent, she felt a rising wave of revulsion. "Would you please open your window?" she asked. "I'd like a little air."

He looked at her, surprised. "Don't you think it's a bit chilly?" But he did roll down the window an inch or so.

Lauren looked around. While she was preoccupied with thoughts of her father, Bell had been driving in the wrong direction. "I forgot that you don't know where I live," she said. "We'll have to turn around."

He shook his head. "I've got a better idea. A friend of mine has a nice secluded place outside of town. He's gone away for a couple of weeks, and he gave me the key to the house."

"That's nice," Lauren said, fighting down her fear, trying to keep her voice normal, "but I really can't. I—I have a class in the morning."

"So do I, remember?" He chuckled softly. "It's not that late. Only ten o'clock."

Lauren's mind was racing. They were already out of the downtown area. The streets were getting darker and the few buildings were far apart. She twisted her head to look out the rear window. There were no cars behind them. Could Kobelski possibly be there without her knowing it?

Of course he could, she told herself, battling a steadily growing feeling of panic. He was a professional. Why, he'd been watching her for a week, and she'd never once spotted him.

But that was different—she had followed a regular routine. If he lost her, he always knew where he could pick up her trail again. But how could he know about Professor Bell's friend's house?

She tried to think of the situation objectively. Bell couldn't be planning to kill her, she reassured herself. Too many people had seen them together this evening.

An unpleasant thought occurred to her. Would he rape her if she weren't cooperative? He was supposed to be violent. And what did he have to fear? Even if she charged him with rape, who'd believe *her*? Especially after all those people had seen her with him earlier? He certainly hadn't forced her to eat or drink with him.

There was something else to consider, too. If Bell were the murderer they were after, he might not ever have actually planned to kill. It might have been an impulsive reaction to—to what?—a rejection of his advances?

"I don't feel very well," she said. "I—I'd appreciate it if you'd take me home now."

He looked at her angrily. "Listen! This evening was *your* idea! Don't——" He stopped abruptly and smiled. "You're probably just a little tense. Perhaps a dip in my friend's heated pool will relax you."

"But I don't have a suit," Lauren said nervously.

He chuckled softly. "That's all right. I'm not bashful." The arm he had around her shoulder tightened. "Don't be frightened," he said softly. "This will be pleasant. I've been told I'm very good."

Oh boy! Lauren thought. There had to be a way out of this situation, and she'd better find it, fast.

The road was dark and tree-lined. There was no sign of another car anywhere. The few houses they passed were dark. She couldn't let Bell get to his friend's house, and she had no idea how much farther it was. If only she could stop the car and push him out!

Wait a minute. She *could* stop the car.

"Professor Bell?"

He turned to her with a little smile. "Don't you think you should call me Warren?"

She snuggled against his side. "Warren, I've been thinking," she said softly. "This could be fun." She placed a hand gingerly on his thigh.

He smiled at her, obviously pleased and surprised. "Well——"

Lauren took advantage of his distraction and slipped her toe up beneath the dashboard. She found the toggle switch and flipped it. The engine, suddenly without gas, sputtered and died.

"Damn!" Bell frowned. "What's the matter? Isn't your gas gauge working?"

"We should have plenty of gas," Lauren said innocently. "I filled up earlier this evening." She hesitated. "I'll bet it's that thing under the hood again."

"*What* thing?" He was irritated.

"I'm not sure what it's called, but this happened to me once before." Lauren shrugged. "The man from the service station just wiggled something under the hood and it started right up."

Bell cursed under his breath. "All right. I'll see what I can do. I don't suppose you have a flashlight?"

When she shook her head, he muttered something about women and cars.

As soon as he was out of the car, Lauren rolled up his window and locked both doors. When he realized what she was doing, he began pounding on the door. Through the closed window, she heard him shout hoarsely, "What the hell is this?"

She flipped off the toggle switch, but as she started the motor, Bell stepped in front of the car and reached for the catch on the hood. He knew she wouldn't deliberately run him down, and once he got the hood up, she wouldn't be able to drive away.

Her heart pounding, Lauren threw the car into reverse and jerked away from him. But the road was too dark and narrow for her to turn around. She had to go forward.

Bell was lunging toward the hood again. Desperately, she put the car in neutral and gunned the motor.

Startled, Bell jumped to the side as she had hoped he would. Shifting quickly into driving gear, Lauren floored the gas pedal and shot past him, her tires squealing.

Bell was left behind in the darkness, waving his fists in the air and shouting.

When Lauren looked back in the rearview mirror, she saw a pair of headlights flash on in the distance. Kobelski?

It had to be. Who else would have followed them without headlights? For a moment, she felt regret. Maybe she'd botched things up. Bell would certainly never ask her out again. If he were the killer, she'd just lost the chance to prove it. She bit her lip. There was no sense in worrying about a mistake that was already made. She drove on, turning at the first crossroad she came to, hoping that her sense of direction was good enough to get her home in a roundabout way.

She had just spotted the lights of the city when she realized that she could no longer see the car behind her. Had Kobelski lost her? Or had he simply dropped back into invisibility now that he knew she was safe?

She was inserting the key into the lock of her apartment door when it occurred to her that if Kobelski had been following her, he wouldn't have had a chance to check out her apartment before she got home. Now what?

Lauren had noticed as she approached the building that the lights were still on in Miss Emerson's apartment. When she knocked on the door, Miss Emerson appeared still fully dressed. In one hand she held a pillowcase that she'd evidently been embroidering.

"Yes, dearie?"

"I'm sorry to bother you at this hour," Lauren said. "But I wondered—would you stay here in the hall for a couple of minutes while I check to make sure there's no one in my apartment?"

Miss Emerson looked alarmed. "Oh, dear! Did you see someone in there?"

"Actually, no," Lauren tried to reassure her. "I'm just a little nervous."

Miss Emerson clucked. "Better safe than sorry. I'll stay right here."

Leaving her door wide open, Lauren turned on all the lights and methodically checked every conceivable hiding place. It took only a couple minutes to assure herself that no one was there. Still, she felt uneasy. She paused. Had Kobelski been here earlier? Was this the same feeling she'd had before—the sense of an alien presence? Or was it just nerves?

She turned back to the hall to tell Miss Emerson that everything was all right. The little woman smiled at her. "Good! Now we'll both sleep better." She quietly closed her door.

Lauren stood in the hall, staring. Had Miss Emerson been holding something under that partially embroidered pillowcase? And was it only her imagination that made her think that the object was a gun?

CHAPTER TWENTY-SIX

Lots of people who live alone keep a gun for protection, Lauren told herself. There wasn't anything unusual about that. If Miss Emerson really had been holding a gun.

Anyhow, Lauren had more important things to think about. Professor Bell would probably flunk her after what had happened tonight. And that would be the end of her education, her career—all her plans. Her life was getting more and more confused.

Kobelski arrived a few minutes later. He wore a black long-sleeved sweater and dark pants, perfect attire for someone who wished to remain inconspicuous on a dark night.

"You okay?" He glanced around the room.

She nodded.

He looked tired. His eyes were bloodshot and he badly needed a shave. He sat down at the table in the kitchenette and rubbed his eyes with both hands.

"I—I guess I goofed things up tonight, huh?" she asked.

He shook his head, mustering a mirthless smile. "No, you did fine. You were smart to get rid of Bell when you did. Where in hell was he taking you, anyway?"

She explained. "I wasn't sure you could protect me there. I thought I'd better take control of the situation myself." She pulled out the matching kitchen chair and sat opposite him. "Kobelski, do you think Professor Bell is our man?"

He looked away. "It doesn't matter what I think," he said irritably. "We'll know for sure when he makes his move."

"It seems to me that we never quite give him a chance

to,'' Lauren said quietly. ''This could go on forever, and I'm getting tired of it.''

He jerked his head up and looked at her with narrowed eyes. ''What's wrong? Can't you take it anymore?''

''I'm not sure I want to. I've never in my life been so scared as I was tonight when Bell started driving out of town.''

''Yes,'' Kobelski admitted, ''he threw you quite a curve. But you handled it all right.''

''This time! But maybe next time——'' She sighed and buried her face in her hands. ''I'm not cut out for this, Kobelski,'' she said tiredly. ''I'm always looking over my shoulder, suspecting everybody. And I'm tired of being watched all the time.''

''I didn't know I was being so obvious.''

''You aren't. It's everyone else! Paul at the lab and Professor Bell. Even Miss Emerson kind of spies on me and so does her nephew.'' She stopped. ''I forgot to tell you about him.''

He looked at her quizzically. ''Who's that?''

''Miss Emerson's nephew. His name's Andrew.''

He looked puzzled. ''What does he look like?''

''He's about twenty-five. Medium height and coloring. Long narrow face. I've noticed him watching me several times in different places.''

She couldn't tell from his expression what he was thinking. ''I'll look into it,'' he said. ''Don't worry. Anything else?''

''Paul's disappeared and that really bothers me. He's desperate, and I'm afraid he'll hurt someone—or himself.''

''Why are you so concerned?''

''I feel responsible. Don't you see? If I hadn't made myself look like Ellen, he wouldn't have gone to pieces the way he did.''

''That's nonsense!'' Kobelski snapped. ''It started when the police questioned him.''

''But he muddled through that all right. He didn't crack up until I——''

The phone rang. She went into the bedroom to answer it.

"Oh, so you're finally home!" Aunt Lil's tone was scathing.

"How is Ma?"

"Doped up and sleeping."

"Then she's still at home?" Lauren's heart was in her throat. "Didn't you put her in the hospital? Didn't you get the money?" She'd forgotten to ask Kobelski whether he'd sent it.

"Oh, she's in the hospital, all right. Bayview General. And the money came, just like you promised."

"Oh, that's good."

"*Is* it? Where does a girl like you get five thousand dollars at the drop of a hat?"

"Five thou——" Lauren looked at the door to the other room.

"*Where did you get it, girl?*"

Lauren swallowed. "I—I borrowed it."

"Hmph! Not from a bank, you didn't!"

How did she know? "No. I—I borrowed it from—my boss." That was true, in a way.

"What's his name?" Aunt Lil shot back.

Lauren hesitated.

"I thought you wouldn't say! I knew there was something fishy going on! Western Union said they couldn't tell me who sent the money. If this is all aboveboard, why does your boss want to remain anonymous?"

Lauren had no answer.

"And what does a girl have to do to get her boss to lend her that kind of money?"

"Aunt Lil! I haven't done anything wrong! I borrowed the money and I'll repay it. That's all you need to know."

"You can't buy your Ma's health with dirty money! What you should do is come and stay with her. She's real upset that you're not here."

Lauren groaned. "I can't come now. Maybe in a while—I don't know. Just make sure she gets everything she needs. Please!"

"Hmph!" Aunt Lil banged down the receiver at the other end of the line.

Lauren was trembling with anger as she returned to the kitchenette, where Kobelski was making two cups of instant coffee. He turned to her. "Want some?"

"*Five thousand dollars*, Kobelski! Does Mr. Rickover know about that?"

He flushed. "Let me worry about it."

"What are you trying to do? Make me feel so obligated that I have to do whatever you say? That's blackmail!"

"It wasn't meant to be," he said softly. "I just don't want you to worry about your mother, that's all."

"She thinks I've abandoned her."

"We've been over all this." His jaw set into a grim line. "You can't leave!"

"But——"

"She's being taken care of." He motioned for Lauren to sit down and set a cup of coffee in front of her.

"Damn it, Kobelski! There are some things money can't buy!"

For just an instant, his eyes had a fierce look. A moment later he was able to say very calmly, "It's hard on you, I know."

"Oh, you don't know the half of it!" she said bitterly. "Warren Bell will certainly do his best—or worst—to see that I flunk his course. My aunt thinks I'm a tramp. And, for that matter, so does everyone else who saw me tonight, even——"

"Joe College?" His tone was sardonic.

"I've hurt him, Kobelski. Can't I at least explain to *him*?"

"No way." He drained the rest of his coffee.

"But——"

"Sorry, doll." He shook his head emphatically. "We've got to play it straight, even if it hurts." His expression softened. "Look, if he cares about you half as much as you seem to care about him, what happened tonight won't stop him. Give him a chance to cool off."

"Maybe you're right," she agreed hesitantly. "And what about Paul?"

"We're trying to catch a killer," Kobelski said coldly. "And if Paul is an innocent victim, he's that killer's victim, not yours!"

"I still don't like it." Lauren toyed with her cup, which was still full of coffee, now half-cold. "I feel as if I've been caught in a whirlpool and the water's closing over my head."

"You can't quit!"

"I know. I owe Mr. Rickover a great deal of money. You made sure of that!"

"I told you the money's not important to him."

"But I can't just take it."

"Then earn it!" he bellowed savagely.

She was too startled by his anger to reply.

He glowered at her. "Well?"

She sighed resignedly and buried her face in her hands.

"Follow your normal routine tomorrow," he said curtly. "Let's see how Bell reacts toward you now."

He rose to rinse out his cup and she looked up. "What about Paul?"

He hesitated. "I have a hunch where he might be. Don't worry. If he's innocent, we'll straighten things out."

"It may not be that simple!" she said angrily. "If he's really cracked up, all of Mr. Rickover's money isn't going to 'straighten things out'!"

He grinned. "Get a good night's sleep, Lauren. You'll feel better in the morning." He started for the door.

"Kobelski?"

"Yeah?" He looked back at her.

"I hate you."

His expression did not change. "I know."

CHAPTER TWENTY-SEVEN

Lauren stared at the spiderweb of cracks in her bedroom ceiling, which the morning sunlight threw into high relief.

Men are all monsters, she thought. Kobelski was using her. And Professor Bell! He was a first-class bastard if there ever was one. But it was Terry who had really disappointed her. Dear funny, gentle Terry. There had been undisguised contempt in his eyes last night. She punched up her pillow. He had called her a bitch and then walked off.

She squinted at the cracks on the ceiling as if she suddenly saw a new and clearer pattern. He had turned his back on her and walked away. Just like Daddy had.

Think how Ma must have felt! Maybe she hadn't driven him away. Perhaps there had been an equally foolish misunderstanding between them. Or maybe Daddy had been quick-tempered or immature. Lauren had never once admitted that her father might have had faults, that her mother's complaints might have some basis in reality. Poor Ma!

Lauren looked at the clock. Seven-ten. It would be eight-ten in Florida. Hospital patients were never allowed to sleep late, were they? She reached for the phone and began dialing.

"Laurie? Is that you?" Ma's voice sounded clearer, stronger.

"How are you feeling? Did they give you a decent room?"

"The room is real pretty, honey." As usual, Ma ignored the personal question. "And I've got a nice roommate, too. A girl your age. Her baby died and she's been very depressed."

Lauren was glad her mother was sharing a room. Besides

191

saving money, it would give her less chance to be alone and start brooding.

"She reminds me of you, Laurie. I wish you were here."

Lauren bit her lip. "I wish I could be, Ma. And I will come as soon as I can get away. But right now——"

"I know. You've got your job, and school, too. I don't want you to get behind in school, Laurie."

"Don't worry about it, Ma. Just get better, okay?"

"I'll be all right. It's just that——" Ma cleared her throat and was silent for a moment. When she found her voice, she said, "I know I said a lot of bad things about your father, but he didn't deserve to die alone."

For a moment neither of them said anything.

Lauren drew a deep breath. "Ma, I—I think I understand how much this hurts. I never understood before. I haven't been fair to you."

A sob. "It's all right, baby. You had to believe in him. Little girls always need to believe in their fathers."

"And their mothers, too. I've got a good one," Lauren said softly. "I guess I haven't appreciated her."

"Do you mean that, Laurie?"

"Yes, Ma. I'm sorry I never said that before."

There was a long silence. Finally, Ma said, "It was my fault. I sent him away."

Lauren's heart sank. "You *what?*"

"I told him that if he didn't change, he shouldn't come home anymore. We'd quarreled so much. He never worked steady, you know."

"Ma, what—what kind of work did he do?"

A little strangled laugh came over the line. "As little as possible, usually."

Lauren was impatient. "Yes, but what?"

"Anything that came along." Her mother thought for a moment. "He sold pots and pans for a while. Then he was a janitor in an office building, a night clerk in a hotel. There were so many jobs. He never kept one long."

"But what kind of a job kept him on the road?"

Her mother was silent for a few moments. Then she said in a low voice, "Sometimes, when he lost a job—or quit one—he'd be ashamed to come home and tell me. So he'd just—go away for a few days." She paused. "I didn't want the neighbors to know. So I'd tell them that he was on the road."

Lauren closed her eyes. There was the end of that fantasy. The only thing extraordinary about her father had been his weaknesses. He was nothing like she'd imagined.

"I never thought he'd *stay* away," Ma was saying in an unsteady voice. "I figured he'd change. I tried to force him. You can't change a man, Laurie. He is what he is."

"I know." Lauren thought of Doug.

"You've always blamed me, haven't you?"

"I didn't understand, Ma. It's okay now. Just concentrate on getting well."

"Mmm. Nurse is here with my pills."

"I'll call again in a couple of days."

A second after she hung up the receiver, the phone rang. "Lauren? Please let me talk to you." It was Terry.

Lauren was tempted to say that there was nothing to talk about, but she held her tongue.

"I'm sorry for what I said last night. I had no right to. I guess I was making jealous noises, and that's pretty prehistoric."

"Terry, I wish I could explain."

"That's what I'm trying to say, Lauren. You don't need to explain. I know looks can be deceiving, and I trust you. Trust requires no explanation, does it?"

"No."

"Then if you'll forgive me for that outburst last night I'd like to forget the whole thing."

Lauren smiled. "Me, too. It's forgotten."

"I hope you haven't made any other plans for tomorrow night."

"No, I haven't."

"Good! Give me a chance to make up for hurting you."

As she hung up, Lauren felt a little guilty. After all, she had hurt him, too. If only she could tell him the truth! How long would it be?

She suddenly remembered Kobelski's saying to her, "Look, you can still get out! You don't have to go through with this!" He was perfectly serious at the time. That had been only last Wednesday. Early Thursday morning, actually. And yet, a few hours later he had insisted that she could not possibly go to her mother.

In just a couple of hours on Thursday morning, something had made him change his mind. Come to think of it, he'd been especially uptight since then. She'd noticed the difference in him.

What does he know that I don't?

CHAPTER TWENTY-EIGHT

During the cytology lecture, Warren Bell appeared to be his usual self. He brushed a thread from the sleeve of his cable-knit sweater and cleared his throat. "Today we're going to discuss the process of cloning. That is, the production from somatic cells of many genetically identical individuals. This, of course, has already been done in some lower animals. Applying the process to humans raises some very complex legal and ethical questions."

Lauren took notes quickly. She had deliberately chosen a seat at the back of the room, and not once during his lecture did Bell look at her. Just before the end of the class period, he passed back the tests they had taken on Wednesday.

"Almost everyone did quite well," he announced. "I think you've proved that you can cover about twice as much material for the next exam."

The students groaned, then laughed nervously as they realized that he was smiling.

Lauren waited as he handed back the tests to all the other students. But there was no paper for her. The bell sounded and everyone got up, scraping chairs against the floor, shuffling books and papers. As they began filing out of the lecture hall, Lauren hurried up the aisle to catch Professor Bell before he left through the side door.

"Professor Bell," she said uncomfortably, "I didn't get my test back."

He looked at her indifferently. "Perhaps that's because you didn't take the exam."

Lauren flushed with anger. "But I *did!* You know I did!"

The few students who had not yet left the room eyed them curiously.

"Well, if you took the test," he said softly, "you should have handed it in. I can't give you a grade unless I see the exam."

"I *did* hand it in," she said evenly, trying to control her increasing fury. "I gave it to you! You were standing right by that door!"

"Impossible," Bell said coolly. "If you had, it would have been with the other test papers. And it wasn't."

So that was the game he was going to play. Lauren stared at him. "What do you suggest I do?"

He smiled thinly. "Since you have no good excuse for not handing in your exam, by rights you should take a zero. However, out of the goodness of my heart—and because you have been doing good work until now—I will allow you to take a makeup exam. It will be a different exam, of course. It wouldn't be fair to give you the same exam, as you already know the questions that were asked."

Lauren's heart sank. She could imagine what the makeup exam would be like. He could make it impossibly subjective, so that no matter how she answered he could argue that her answers weren't complete enough to warrant a passing grade. On the other hand, if she refused to take a makeup, he could give her a zero. How could she prove that she'd given him her exam paper? Nedra knew that she had taken the exam, of course, but could Nedra *swear* that Lauren had handed the paper in? Could anyone in the class remember seeing her do it?

All the other students had gone. They were alone in the lecture hall. Lauren drew a deep breath. "I am not going to take a makeup exam," she said slowly, "because I've already taken this exam, and you have my paper. Either you give me the grade I earned, or I'm going to the board of regents."

Bell smiled. "What makes you think they'll believe you? I'm sure they'll realize that this is simply a case of spite on your part because I no longer choose to see you on a personal basis."

"You don't choose——" Lauren nearly choked. "All

right. Maybe they won't believe *me*. But I'll find some other girls you've treated like this—and I know there are quite a few. The regents will find it hard to believe that *all* of us are lying!''

He paled. ''You wouldn't dare!''

''Oh, yes, I would!'' she challenged him. ''If I don't have a grade—a fair grade—by Monday morning, you are in for some real trouble, *Professor* Bell!''

He glared at her. His blue eyes were cold with hatred. ''We'll see!''

Lauren swallowed as she left the lecture hall. She was sorely tempted to skip her laboratory session. The thought of spending another two hours in the same room with the man was repulsive. But she wasn't going to give him any concrete reason to lower her grade. She would go to lab and do her experiment in spite of him.

But to her surprise and relief, Warren Bell did not show up for the laboratory session. The students, unperturbed, went about their work, relying on each other for help when it was needed.

As Lauren unlocked her cabinet and began assembling the materials for the day's experiment, Nedra, her dark eyes wide with curiosity, edged up to her. ''What happened last night?'' she whispered.

In a low voice, Lauren told her. ''He's trying to get even with me by flunking me on the test,'' she finished.

Nedra shook her head. ''I don't understand why you went out with him in the first place. In a way, you asked for it.''

It was Kobelski who had asked for it, Lauren thought tiredly.

''What are you going to do now?'' Nedra asked.

When Lauren explained, the girl stared at her in admiration. ''You've got guts, I'll say that for you!''

''Guts and desperation go together,'' Lauren said sourly.

''Well, if it comes to the worst, I can give you the names of a few girls who can help you.''

''Thanks. I hope I won't need them.''

''You may not. I think you've shaken him up.''

"Why do you say that?"

Nedra looked around the room. "Because I've *never* heard of him skipping out on a class before."

When she got to work that afternoon, Lauren found that none of the blood samples they had reordered had yet arrived.

"You may as well take the day off," Dr. Herbert told her. "Heaven knows you deserve it after this week!"

Lauren looked at him gratefully. A day off! She knew just what she wanted to do. Shop for something special to wear to Terry's party tomorrow night. Something soft and silky that would make Terry sit up and take notice.

Four hours later, she had purchased a pale-gray pantsuit with a smashing red satin blouse. A pair of matching gray shoes completed the outfit. She'd had her hair done, too. It renewed her spirits and bolstered her courage for tonight's confrontation with Doug.

She was feeling considerably better as she walked toward the parking garage where she'd left her car. She glanced at her watch. It was just after five. Even if she stopped for a hamburger on the way home—she had not eaten any lunch—there would still be time for a nap before Doug made his appearance. It seemed like forever since she'd had a good night's sleep.

"Hey, Lauren! Wait up!" Pudge was winding his way through the traffic. He puffed up to her. "Did Terry get hold of you yet?" he asked.

Lauren looked at him. It was really none of his business. "He called me this morning," she said tentatively.

"Everything okay between you two now?" His expression showed such genuine concern that Lauren couldn't feel offended.

"Yes, it is." She smiled at him.

"Good!" He fell into step beside her. "Our place was like a morgue last night. It was bad enough about Kelso and Angie, but you and Terry, too." He shook his head. "I probably shouldn't say this, but he really has flipped out

over you. Do you know, he paced the floor all night?''
Pudge kicked at a stone on the sidewalk. ''I told him that he
shouldn't jump to conclusions. I mean, so you had a beer
with Big Bad Bell! So what!''

Lauren colored, but Pudge seemed oblivious to her discomfort. ''I mean, anyone who'd met you could tell you
weren't the kind of girl who'd——'' He stopped and
flushed. ''I suffer from a terrible disease,'' he said awk-
wardly. ''Foot in mouth.''

Lauren laughed. ''It's all right, Pudge. I understand what
you're trying to say. And thanks for coming to my
defense.''

Pudge stuck his hands in his pockets. ''You're one nice
lady, you know that? And I'm glad Terry's come to his
senses.''

''Me, too. Did he really pace the floor all night?''

''Well, half of it, anyhow. Terry's like that. When he's
got a problem, he wrestles with it by himself until he comes
to a solution. At least nobody else has to suffer with him.
Kelso's completely different. After he and Angie had that
fight, I had to listen to his side of the story for three hours.
Then he got one of his headaches and locked himself in his
room for a whole day. He'd come out every once in a while
and yell at us for making too much racket. It's only now that
he's coming back to normal.''

An automobile horn honked nearby. They turned to see
Foxy Freddy driving Kelso's MG. He pulled up alongside a
fire hydrant and waited for them.

''Hi, Lauren,'' he greeted her. To Pudge, he said, ''I've
been looking all over for you. You'd better come home,
fast.''

''What's up?''

''It's Kelso, and he's down.''

''Oh-oh. Did Angie call him again?''

''Worse than that. The police were over today.''

Pudge looked surprised. ''What did he *do?* Who called
the police?''

A look of impatience crossed Freddy's round face. ''Nobody called them. They're questioning him again. It seems there's something wrong with his alibi for the weekend Dee Dee was killed.''

Pudge paled. ''He doesn't think I said anything to the police, does he? Hey, I was only kidding!''

''I don't know what Kelso thinks,'' Freddy said. ''But now the police want to know where he was when the other girl was killed.

Pudge snorted. ''They're crazy! Anybody who knows Kelso would know that he wouldn't——''

''Well, of course not,'' Freddy agreed.

''Exactly what happened when the police came?'' Lauren asked quickly.

''Not a whole lot, really. When they started asking questions, Kelso called his father. Then his father called his lawyer, and the lawyer said Kelso should not say anything. Well, there wasn't much the police could do, so they left. But Kelso's feeling really low. Imagine how you'd feel if the police were trying to pin a murder on you!''

''Yeah.'' Pudge climbed into the small car and looked back at Lauren. ''Do you need a ride back to campus? Of course, with only two seats, you'd have to sit on my lap.'' He looked at her hopefully.

Lauren laughed. ''My car's in the parking garage in the next block. Thanks anyway.''

CHAPTER TWENTY-NINE

Doug arrived promptly at ten. Lauren braced herself before answering the door. She was wearing her new gray and red outfit. She had planned to save it for Terry, but this was one time Doug's expensive clothes would not intimidate her. She felt a guilty satisfaction, knowing that she would be as well-dressed as he.

Doug looked particularly handsome this evening, she thought. He wore a rust-colored Harris tweed suit, obviously custom-made. "Hello, Lauren. I'm back." His manner was boyishly shy, and Lauren felt a twinge of compassion, sensing the eagerness in his voice.

"Have a seat," she said, feeling awkward. How did one begin a conversation like this?

"You look especially pretty tonight," he said softly. "I hope it's because of me."

She winced inwardly as she sat down. *Yes, it is, Doug,* she thought. *But not for the reasons that you think. It's to give me enough confidence to resist you.* Aloud, she said, "In a way."

He seemed to relax at that, and Lauren realized she had raised his hopes. That wasn't fair. But before she could say anything, Doug was telling her, "I thought you might like to know—Dad says the legal work on the settlement won't take much longer. He thinks we can have a final decree in three or four months. So I'm not asking you to wait long."

Enthusiasm was building in his voice and she knew all too well how easy it was to get caught up in his fervor. If she didn't tell him now, she might lose her nerve. "Doug, I'm not going to wait for you," she said softly.

"*What?*" Disbelief showed in his face. "But I

201

thought—I told you it's all right with me if you want a career."

"It's not only that——"

"Then what?" Distress made his voice crack.

She couldn't very well tell him that deep down inside, she was afraid he would abandon her if the going got rough. Instead, she said, "We're like oil and water, Doug. We just don't belong together. It wouldn't work last year, and it won't work now."

He straightened up a little and a defensive note came into his voice. "What does that mean?"

She stared at the travel poster on the wall behind his head. It showed an Alpine valley strewn with wildflowers. At that moment she felt as far away from Doug as the mountains were from her cramped little apartment. "Sooner or later we're bound to have disagreements," she began.

"No, we won't. Why should we?"

Wrong answer, Doug, she thought with a pang. *You should have said, "We'll work them out together."* Aloud, she said, "You're being unrealistic. No two people can agree all of the time."

"You're the one who's being unrealistic, Lauren. What more can you ask? I've already offered you anything you want."

"Anything that money can buy, you mean?"

"Of course!" He failed to catch the sardonic note in her voice. "Listen, I've got it all planned! A friend of Dad's owns a townhouse right here in the city. I think we can get a good deal on it. You can go to school, just as you wanted." He paused and leaned forward, his face becoming more animated as he spoke. "And listen to this: I've found out that Dad knows a few people on the faculty here. You know, a nice donation to the Alumni Fund——"

"I prefer to *earn* my degree," she said coldly.

"Of course, of course." He spoke hurriedly, trying to hide his confusion by bending down and wiping an invisible spot from the tip of one freshly shined shoe. "But it doesn't hurt to eliminate a little of the red tape, does it?"

He gave her his most winning smile.

She shook her head. "You're a natural salesman, you know that?"

The smile widened. "Then you *will*—"

"No." Her reply was barely audible and Doug furrowed his brow as if he couldn't believe he'd heard her correctly. Lauren swallowed. Her throat was dry, her hands strangely cold. "No," she repeated firmly.

A hurt look shadowed his face. "But *why?* I don't understand."

"That's exactly why," she said. "You don't understand *me!* Oh, Doug! You need a wife you can pamper and protect." She hesitated. "Someone who'll do the same for you in return."

He straightened a little. A glimmer of hope came into his face. "Yes."

"Don't you see? I'm used to doing things for myself. I like it that way! Otherwise I feel *smothered!*"

He stared at her with a hurt expression on his face. "You never said these things before."

"Because I didn't realize——" She searched for the right words. There was really nothing more to say. "Your parents were right all along, Doug."

"No!" His eyes clouded with anger.

"Yes, they were. I'd never fit in with your family and friends."

"You'd learn! In no time at all, you'll feel like one of the family."

Lauren suddenly remembered an incident at their engagement party. Doug's sister, Marcia, had come up to her as Lauren was talking with several people.

"Hello, Lauren," she had gushed. "Is that a new dress? Wherever did you get it?"

"Oh, at Grummond's," she'd answered and then bit her lip as she saw the look of amusement on the faces around her. The Martins and their friends did not buy clothing from department stores.

Marcia had smiled knowingly. "*Really!* Imagine that!"

At the time, Lauren had felt embarrassed and humiliated. Now, remembering the incident, she felt angry. Wealth was no excuse for rudeness. But Doug's people had never learned that. They probably never would.

"I don't *want* to be one of the family, Doug." As soon as she had spoken, she regretted her choice of words.

Amazement, hurt and anger flashed in Doug's dark eyes. "Do you realize what I'm offering you? An escape"—he looked around the room with contempt—"from *this!* You'll have a beautiful home, clothes, jewelry. We'll travel, go to the finest places. You'll be an important person."

She couldn't resist. "That's funny. I thought I already was."

He glowered. Finally, in exasperation, he said, "All right! What *do* you want?"

Love, Doug, she thought. *You never even mentioned love.* She sighed. "There really isn't any use going over all this again. We're very different people, Doug. We live in different worlds."

He looked away. "Okay," he said resignedly. "I know when I've lost a sale."

Leave it to Doug, she thought, *to compare a proposal to a sales pitch.* She stood up and followed him to the door.

"One thing, before I leave," he said.

"What's that?"

"This past year—haven't there been times when you regretted not marrying me?"

She looked up at him. He was trying to salvage some of his pride. "Sometimes." She tried to make her voice sound sincere.

"You're going to regret it this time, too." His voice was bitter. He left without looking back.

How like Doug, she thought. Lashing back at her because he didn't get his way. It was understandable, though. She was probably the only person in his life who had ever refused him anything. And she'd done it twice.

Kobelski showed up a short while later. "Mr. Martin didn't look happy when he left," he commented dryly.

"I don't want to talk about it, Kobelski. It doesn't concern you."

He shrugged his broad shoulders. "Okay. How about some coffee?" He sat down at the table and put his feet up on the other chair. "How'd it go with Bell today?"

"He was really angry," she said as she plugged in the coffee pot. "He's going to try to flunk me." She told him what had happened.

Kobelski let out a low whistle and put his feet down so that she could sit on the other chair. "So you really challenged him, huh? You're getting pretty good at this baiting business."

She felt the blood drain from her face. "I never thought of it that way. You mean he may be angry enough to kill me?"

"If he's our man."

"Do you think he is?"

He ignored her question. "What have you got planned for tomorrow?"

"I am going to sleep all morning. I don't care what you say! I haven't had a decent night's sleep since I met you."

He grinned. "And what are you going to do after you've slept all morning?"

"I'll spend the afternoon studying at the main library. And then in the evening I'm going to a party."

He raised an eyebrow. "Joe College?"

"How'd you know?"

"The way your face lit up when you said you were going to a party." His voice held a sour note.

She stared at him. "Kobelski, are you jealous?"

He ignored her. "Where's the party? And who else will be there?"

"At his apartment. His roommates and their dates will be there. Only eight of us. I won't be terribly visible, will I? Is that what's bothering you?"

The scar stood out on his cheek. "Who says anything's bothering me?"

"*Something* is."

Kobelski didn't reply. He looked at her with such a fierce expression that she became uncomfortable. She changed the subject. "Have you found out anything about Paul?"

"I found out why he was in the mental hospital."

"Why?"

"It seems that he has what is called a weak ego structure. Under stress he just falls apart. Freaks out."

"What did he do?"

"The first time—a couple of years ago—he vandalized the home of a girl who'd broken a date with him."

"But he hasn't harmed anyone, has he?" The coffee had stopped perking. She got up to pour it into their cups.

"He came close the second time. He ran a car off the road because he was convinced that the driver had cut him off at an intersection. Fortunately no one was hurt, and his psychiatrist convinced the judge that Paul should be put in a hospital instead of a jail."

"Then he *is* capable of killing someone," Lauren said slowly.

"Everyone has a breaking point," he said mildly. "It's just that Paul's is very near the surface at times."

"Do you know where he is?" She set his coffee down in front of him.

He shook his head. "No, but I've got a hunch. I'm expecting further information shortly."

"I hope it's not Paul," she said. "I don't want him to be the killer."

"Who would you like it to be?" He was amused.

"I don't want him to be anybody I know."

"Not even Bell?" He sipped his coffee.

"No. He may be a rotten human being, but he's a good teacher, and I have to admire him for that. No, I want the killer to be a stranger."

"Not much chance."

"Well, then someone I don't really know. Like Miss Emerson's nephew. Did you check on him, by the way?"

"Yeah. Nothing there. Likes to watch pretty girls, that's all. Rather shy fellow."

"Well, he's the one I wouldn't want to meet in a dark alley. I wish you'd do a little more checking on Andrew— what's his last name?"

Kobelski frowned. "His last name?"

"You must have it. Look in your notebook."

He pulled his notebook from an inside pocket and thumbed through it. "Yeah, here it is. Curran. Andrew Curran. Age twenty-seven. Part-time student. Otherwise unemployed. No record. No history of trouble."

"Curran," Lauren repeated. "That's funny. It doesn't sound right. I thought Miss Emerson said it was something else." She tried to remember. *Keely? Could it have been Curry?*

Kobelski was watching her. "Problem?"

She shrugged. "Probably not. I'm terrible at remembering names."

He finished his coffee and stood up. "Well, I'm off." He reached over and touched her cheek lightly with his fingertips. "Try to get that extra sleep. You look as though you need it."

She nodded. "I had an hour's nap earlier, but I'm so far behind on sleep. I really don't know how I've managed to function——" She stopped. He was looking at her in an oddly preoccupied way. She was sure he didn't hear a word she was saying. "Kobelski?"

He gave a little start. "Yeah?"

"What were you thinking just now?"

To her surprise, a look of anguish crossed his face. Then he rinsed out his coffee cup and left.

CHAPTER THIRTY

Lauren slept until nearly noon on Saturday. As she showered and dressed she had a nagging feeling of having forgotten something. It wasn't until she gathered her books, preparing to leave for the library, that it came to her. She remembered Miss Emerson standing in the foyer with Andrew. *"I don't believe you've met my nephew, Andrew Neely."* That was what she had said—Neely. It wasn't even close to Curran. Why had Kobelski told her it was Curran? Come to think of it, he'd seemed hesitant about it. But why should he lie to her? Unless he didn't know Andrew's last name. Because he'd never checked up on him at all. *He lied to me before*, she thought uncomfortably.

Lauren set her books back down on the table. A disconcerting thought occurred to her. She didn't really know anything about Kobelski, except what he'd told her. When she first met him, he'd flashed some kind of identification, but she hadn't really paid any attention to it—she'd been so worried about Ma. Besides, identification cards could be forged.

This is silly, she thought. *You're probably worrying about nothing.* But it was easy enough to check up on him. She dialed the police department and asked to speak to Captain Hunnicut. A slightly gruff voice came on the line. "Captain Hunnicut's not in right now. What's this about?"

"It has to do with the Rickover murder case," Lauren said. "Is there someone else who is working on that?"

"I'll connect you with Sergeant Edwards. He's second in command."

Sergeant Edwards had a nasal voice. "Hello, this is Edwards." He took her name and address. "What can I do for you?"

"Do you know the private detective who's working on the Rickover case?" she asked.

He seemed puzzled. "A *private* detective? If you want a private detective, why are you calling *me*?

"He says he stays in touch with you. To keep up with the investigation."

"Oh, really?" Edwards' voice dripped with sarcasm. "And what's this hotshot's name?"

"Ernest Kobelski."

There was a little laugh on the other end of the line. "Ernest *What*-ski? I never heard of him."

"But he mentioned Captain Hunnicut specifically. Is it possible that you didn't know he was working with——"

"Lady," Edwards said with exaggerated patience, "why should Captain Hunnicut keep secrets from me? I don't know who this guy is. Sounds like a conman to me. What's he trying to get you to do?"

Lauren's throat went dry. "Nothing," she said quickly. "It—it's probably a joke." Her heart was pounding as she hung up.

So. The police didn't even know him. He'd lied to her about that. And about what else?

After calling Chicago area information, she dialed Thomas Rickover's number only to hear a bored voice announce, "This is Mr. Rickover's answering service."

"Oh," Lauren said, disappointed. "Can you tell me when Mr. Rickover will be in?"

"He doesn't give me that information," the voice said haughtily. "All I know is that he's away on business right now."

"Then I can't get in touch with him?"

"He calls in from time to time to collect his messages, if you'd like to leave one."

"Thanks, but no." Lauren hung up. There had to be a faster way to check on Kobelski.

She dialed Chicago area information again. "Do you have a listing for Ernest Kobelski?"

Twenty minutes later, she put down the receiver with a

shaking hand. There was no Ernest Kobelski in Chicago nor in any of the suburban listings. The operator had assured her that there was no Ernest Kobelski with an unlisted number, either.

A private detective without a telephone? It was all a lie. Everything he had told her was a lie. But why? Who was Kobelski? And what did he want with her? Why stage this elaborate hoax? And why had he gotten her to change her appearance?

So that you'd look like a victim, she answered herself.

Was that what she was going to be? Not the bait, but the victim? With a shudder, she realized how easily Kobelski could kill her. He could get in and out of her apartment anytime he wanted to. He'd been very careful to make sure that no one had ever seen him here. And how diligently he always washed his coffee cup! A wariness of leaving fingerprints?

If he should kill her, Lauren realized, no one would ever know that there was any connection between the two of them.

CHAPTER THIRTY-ONE

But if Kobelski wanted to kill her, why hadn't he done so already? He'd had plenty of opportunity. She shook her head in confusion. She didn't know how a psychopath's mind worked. That evening in the Nite Owl when they had been discussing the murders, didn't Kelso mention something about a ritualistic pattern? Maybe it was necessary to prepare the victim in a certain way. Like a sacrificial lamb.

Oh, God! Had he done the same thing with Ellen? Had he gone to her and told her he was a detective working on Dee Dee's murder and would Ellen mind playing bait?

Should she call the police? What could they do? Guard her? Against a man who hadn't even threatened her? Against a man who'd given her seven hundred dollars—and then five thousand to care for her sick mother? She'd look worse in their eyes than Kobelski. They'd never believe her.

With a sinking heart, she realized that she couldn't even run away. Kobelski was capable of following her wherever she went without her realizing it.

The phone rang and she went into the bedroom to answer it.

"Hello, gorgeous! Glad I caught you home."

"Terry!"

"I want to take you to dinner tonight before the party."

"Terry, please listen to me. I need your help."

"Hey, what's wrong?"

"I'll explain later. But please, will you do something important for me right now?"

"Name it. I'm the knight on the white horse."

"Oh, Terry, this is *serious*."

213

"I'm all ears." His voice suddenly sobered.

"I want you to go to a hardware store and get a deadbolt lock for my door and the tools to install it. I'll reimburse you when you get here. Could you, as quickly as possible? And you'll have to help me install it."

"Hey, what's going on?"

"Please, Terry. Hurry!"

"It may take a little while to get the stuff," he said slowly. "Will you be all right in the meantime?"

Would she? "I think so."

"I'll be there as fast as I can." Terry said as he hung up.

Lauren looked at the clock. It seemed to have stopped. She sat down in the easy chair with a feeling of helplessness. Why did it seem that every man in her life eventually failed her? Her father had abandoned her; Doug couldn't accept her as she was; Paul had turned against her when she tried to help him. Even Terry, however briefly, had turned away from her. Had she truly forgiven him for that? And now Kobelski. The knowledge that he'd been lying to her all along hurt unbearably.

She glanced at her watch again. It was nearly an hour before Terry arrived, packages under his arm.

"Everything okay?" He looked at her with concern. "Sorry I took so long, but I had to go to two different stores to get everything." He set the packages down on the table and turned to look at her. "Now, don't you think you should tell me what this is all about?"

Lauren hesitated. She was too embarrassed to admit how gullible she'd been. To let a strange man into her apartment, to take his word that he was a detective, to put herself in such a vulnerable position. What stupid things to do! She couldn't tell him that. She shook her head. "It's a long story. Someone is trying to kill me, Terry."

Shock registered on his face. "What! But who? And why?"

"I'm not sure *who* he is," Lauren said. "All I know is that he killed those other two girls, and now he's after me."

She was shaking. Terry took her hands in his and rubbed them. "That's pretty heavy," he said slowly, searching her face. "Are you sure you're not imagining this?"

"Don't you believe me?"

"Have you told the police?"

She shook her head. "What could I say? He hasn't done anything yet! Please, Terry, just put the lock on the door."

He gave her a long look. "Okay, if that's what you want." He started opening the packages.

"Will it take long?"

He shook his head. "I'm a pretty good handyman. I used to fix a lot of things at home."

"Can I help?"

"Uh-uh." He waved her away. "Too many hands in a small area. You just sit down and stay cool."

It was obviously a bigger job than he'd anticipated. As he struggled with the lock, trying to hold it in position while he tightened the screws, beads of perspiration formed on his temples.

Finally it was done. He tested it twice. "There you are," he said.

Lauren inspected it.

"That's a solid lock," he said. "Feel better?"

"Oh, yes. Thank you, Terry." Impulsively, she hugged him.

But he didn't respond. Instead, he regarded her coolly. *Bad move*, she thought. *He still hasn't forgotten about Thursday night. I really ought to let him make the first move.*

She bent to pick up the wrappings. "I'm awfully grateful for your help." She turned to put them into the wastebasket. "I don't know what I'd have done without you."

"My mother always said that."

There was an odd note in his voice, she thought. Then she heard the footstep behind her and realized that she'd turned her back on him. Before she could turn around, his hands were at her throat. As she felt the pressure of his fingers cutting off her breath, Lauren thought, *Oh, God! I'm going to die!*

She struggled, trying to pry his fingers loose, but he was too strong. Her lungs began to burn. It was hard to stay on her feet. Her body wanted to crumple to the floor. Then, from deep within her, she felt determination rising. She wouldn't give up without a fight.

She jammed the edge of her heel against his instep. The pain caused him to release his grip momentarily, and she whirled around to face him. She drew a painful breath and tried to scream, but only a rasping whisper came out.

Terry was lunging toward her, his normally wide clear eyes glittering with hatred.

"No!" she gasped. "Terry, *why*?"

"You know why, you little whore!" He spat the words at her. His face was strangely contorted.

I've got to keep him talking, she thought desperately. leaning against the wall, trying to keep from falling. "But why Ellen?" She forced the words out with pain.

He hesitated. "Ellen?" His eyes clouded for a moment. "She was evil."

"Evil?" Lauren repeated dully.

"She asked me to her apartment. She said she wanted to draw a picture of me." He frowned. "But when I walked in, I saw that she had drawings of naked people hanging on the walls. Then I knew what she was."

"And Dee Dee?" Lauren slowly edged toward the record player, hoping he was too distracted to notice.

"She was evil, too. I saw how she flaunted her body. I heard what the guys said about her when she sang." His voice dropped to a murmur. "I met her on the street one night and walked her home. She invited me in." He looked at his hands. "*I knew——*"

"And you tore up the music?" She was nearly to the record player now.

"It was a filthy song. She shouldn't have sung it."

"Other girls sing it."

He frowned. "But *she* had no right. *She* shouldn't have——" His frown deepened. "And *you* shouldn't have done what you did."

"If you kill me," she said, trying to make her cracking voice firm, "they'll know it was you. Lots of people know that you've been seeing me."

Incredibly he chuckled. "It's all right. Don't you see? They'll *understand!*"

His eyes were clear again and strangely vacant. Lauren realized that he wasn't even seeing her.

"Why does it always have to be like this?" He almost sobbed. "Why can't any of you be good?" He moved toward her and Lauren made a dive toward the record player. She seized the potted fern and hurled it at the window with all her strength.

As the glass shattered, Terry's hands were at her throat again.

Go for the eyes, she told herself. *Jam your thumbs in his eyes. It's your only chance!*

As she gasped for breath, struggling to get her hands to his face, she kept seeing his eyes the way they were before. His friendly laughing eyes. She gritted her teeth as her thumbs found their mark.

He pulled back in pain and she gulped for air. A bell was ringing shrilly nearby. There were voices in the hall. And loud noises.

He was choking her again and she fought to get her hands back to his face. Dimly she realized that someone was banging at the door. Banging? No, chopping!

Got to stay conscious.

They struggled again and then, abruptly, it was over.

"Let her go!"

Terry's hands released her and Lauren crumpled into a corner of the room.

Miss Emerson was there. The gun she held with both hands was trained on Terry, who cringed on the floor. Andrew, standing beside her, had a gun too.

And Kobelski, towering over Terry, his face fierce and terrible to see, his ragged scar glistening—Kobelski held a fire ax above his head. *"You bastard!"*

Andrew shouted, *"Tom! No!"*

Instantly, Kobelski seemed to deflate. Lowering the ax, he turned away from Terry. "Call the police," he muttered in disgust.

Only then did he appear to notice Lauren huddled in the corner.

CHAPTER THIRTY-TWO

"I just can't believe that you're Thomas Rickover." Lauren's voice was still hoarse.

They were alone in her apartment. The police had taken Terry away. Miss Emerson and Andrew had gone with them.

Kobelski—Thomas Rickover—nodded. A mask had fallen, Lauren realized. There was yet another change in him.

"But *why?* Why didn't you tell me who you were?"

He shook his head. "I couldn't tell anyone. Except Captain Hunnicut, that is. He knew, of course."

"I don't understand."

"A lot of people might not have leveled with me if they knew I was Ellen's father."

"But you *are* a detective?"

"Oh, yes. The head of a rather large agency, as a matter of fact. Miss Emerson—her real name is Margaret Hastings, by the way—and Andy are two of my agents." He grinned at her. "We goofed up on his cover, you know. She gave you one last name and I gave you another."

"I know!" Lauren said. "No wonder she was always poking around and he was following me. They were protecting me, too, weren't they?"

"Uh-huh. We offered Mr. Emerson a paid vacation in exchange for the use of his apartment. It served as a handy base of operations."

Lauren sat down and rubbed her throat.

Rickover frowned. "Perhaps we ought to have a doctor look at you."

She shook her head. "No, it feels a lot better already."

"But you don't."

She did feel strangely depressed. The apartment next door was a "base of operations." Kobelski wasn't Kobelski, Miss Emerson wasn't Miss Emerson, and Andy wasn't her nephew.

And Lauren Walker? Would she ever be the same person again?

"What's wrong?" There was concern in his voice.

"I don't know. I feel so let down."

"And unreal?" He smiled. "We've been playing a part, remember? Actors go through the same thing when a play finishes a long run. It'll wear off."

"I don't even *look* like me anymore! I look like——" She swallowed painfully. "Kobelski—I mean, Mr. Rickover——"

He smiled again. "After all we've been through, I think you should call me Tom."

"Tom"—she hesitated—"there isn't any polite way to ask this, but I have to know. I've got to understand."

"What's that?"

"About Ellen. Why didn't you—I mean——"

Pain shot across his face. "I want you to understand about that. You see, I came here to take her home for burial. But—I couldn't do it." He shook his head. "Ellen and I weren't as close as we should have been. I guess after her mother died, I tried to keep as busy as possible. Too busy."

The fierce look came to his face and the scar on his cheek whitened. "But I loved my daughter, Lauren. I loved her very much. And when I saw her in the morgue——" His eyes glistened and Lauren realized that his fierceness was a cover for other, gentler emotions. He continued softly. "I promised her I'd get him. I couldn't say good-bye to her until I made sure he'd never kill another girl."

"Ko—Tom, I'm sorry. I didn't know what you were going through. I wasn't always very nice to you."

"And I almost got you killed."

"That was my fault. I forgot and turned my back on him."

"I was afraid of that. I knew you trusted him."

"You knew it was Terry, didn't you? That's why you've been acting so differently lately. Why didn't you warn me?"

A pained look came to his face. "I very nearly did."

"Then why didn't you?"

"You're a pretty good actress, Lauren, but not that good."

Lauren considered that. "At any rate, I survived." She thought suddenly of her mother. Would she ever be able to tell her the real reason she hadn't come to Florida? Probably not. If Ma ever knew the truth, she'd only worry more. As for Aunt Lil—well, let her think what she liked.

"I guess we'll all survive," she said. "The only person I feel sorry for is Paul. Did you ever find out what happened to him?"

Rickover nodded. "Knowing his history, I figured he might have gotten in touch with his old psychiatrist after he went berserk in the lab. The doctor wasn't too anxious to talk. He didn't want the police harassing Paul. It took a while, but we finally convinced him that we weren't exactly the police. He told us that Paul submitted to hospitalization Thursday morning."

"I'm sorry. I feel bad about that."

"Paul's doctor told me this would have happened sooner or later. He also says Paul will be all right again."

"There's one more thing," Lauren said. "When did you know that it was Terry?"

"I had a strong hunch as soon as I checked on his background. He fit the profile. His mother wasn't what you'd call a faithful wife. When her husband divorced her, she dumped Terry with her folks and took off. She'd come back between boyfriends."

"That's not what Terry told me. He said his mother always stuck by him."

"Wishful thinking, I guess."

Of course. Terry had lied about his mother the way Lauren had lied about her father. Because the truth had hurt too much. "And his stepfather?" she asked.

"More fantasy, I'm afraid. He probably meant Joe, the man who's been paying his mother's bills for the last ten years. Her married lover."

Lauren winced. "I can see how that would affect an adolescent boy. It must have created a terrific rage within him."

"My guess is that it also made him terrified of female sexuality. But we'll probably never know that for sure."

"Speaking of knowing for sure—what made you sure it was Terry?"

Rickover reached into his inside pocket and pulled a snapshot from his wallet. "I managed to get hold of this yesterday. It's an old picture."

The snapshot showed a little boy and his mother. The boy, perhaps four but already unmistakably Terry, was solemn. The young woman who held him——

Lauren gasped. She might have been looking at herself.

Rickover took her in his arms and held her close. "It's over now," he said softly.

"Ko—Tom?"

"Yeah?"

"I can't hate him. Even now, I feel sorry for him."

His face went hard. "Maybe I'll feel that way, too—someday." He kissed her lightly. "It's time to say goodbye to Ellen. That's something I've got to do alone."

"I know." A flood of emotions washed over her. He was leaving her, too. She felt tears welling in her eyes.

He paused to survey the wreckage of the door. "I'll send someone over to fix this for you," he said.

She nodded numbly.

"And Lauren—"

She looked up.

"If it's all right with you," he said softly, "I'll be back."

Lauren smiled. And then she was laughing and crying at the same time.